WOVEN

INFINITE LOVE

I0684781

A Novella By

Selena Eliona

This book is a work of fiction. The story, all names, characters, and incidents portrayed in this production are of the author's imagination. No identification with actual persons (living or deceased), places, buildings, products, and websites is intended or should be inferred.

Copyright © 2022 by Selena Eliona

For permission request or more information, please visit: **www.SeFeSel.com**.

Paperback ISBN: 978-0-983-8133-0-9
eBook ISBN: 978-0-983-8133-1-6

DEDICATION

This Novella is for Diamond, my Ruby, my Jewel of
Jewels from God.

ACKNOWLEDGEMENTS

I am forever grateful to my daughter who encouraged my writing journey.

Memories shared are never forgotten. I am thankful for every person I ever met.

Most importantly, I thank the MOST HIGH God for my creativity.

CHAPTER ONE

John Watts

The room was filled with grave silence in spite of two people being present there. The clock on the wall raced forward to 10 am, its distinctive ticks and tocks being the only sounds to break the dead silence in between. Both the men in the room were buried in their own thoughts.

There was a recliner in the right corner of the room but John was sitting upright in the chair, his hazel eyes were blazing with fury, there was something disturbing him. Dr. Burke, his military assigned psychiatrist, leaning against the table in front of him, closely observing his facial expressions. The ticking clock kept on its rhythm, trying to remind both men that time is running by and waits for none.

Dr. Burke compared John to a mega-million puzzle. It was impossible to connect one piece to another without extreme patience. Sometimes, a few pieces seemed to connect, only to find that he had made the wrong connection. After all, John worked for one of the highest intelligence agencies in the country. It was his tenth session with Dr. Burke and his mind was still like a secret inexplicable book, which the doctor was trying to read line by line.

1

He had been suffering from PTSD for the last five months and had weekly sessions with Dr. Burke. The emotional need to talk about his horrific, awful experiences with someone made him visit the doctor often. It was clear that he was stuck in a dilemma, a sort of catch-22, where talking about his fears would aggravate them, but the longer he kept them off, the more they affected him.

His condition would usually aggravate after coming back from particular missions and at times he required special counseling sessions. This time, the situation was more intense. It had caused the loss of a loved one, which awoke the furious man inside him.

"What compelled you to join the Agency, John?" asked Dr. Burke. He knew at once it was an intense question for him, a question that hurt him deep down and needed to be probed. He knew that every poke at that beast hurt, and that it could awaken it, but he knew it was necessary.

John's hazel eyes blazed with fury slowly dimmed, he was no longer present there. Instead, he was traveling down memory lane.

He was a fifteen-year-old teenager, whose family was running for their lives. He was having a flashback: his father waking him up in the middle of the night, saying they had to leave their house immediately or all of them would be killed.

John instantly obeyed, grabbing his backpack that his mother threw at him and without asking any typical questions that anyone else would have. There were times when you could ask questions, and times when you would look towards your mother or father and know that you cannot. It was this silent understanding that now was not the time to be a teenager. This time, he knew it was something very serious by looking at his father's stern face.

They used the terrace window in John's bedroom and roped down the back of the home to a jeep parked below. John's dad put the jeep into neutral to roll off in silence before starting the engine. John could hear sirens of military vans near the front gate. "Are they following us?" he thought to himself. It was the only question that he could actually form in his head.

There were many others, but they were all such a mess that he could not focus on one. Right now, he was here, and the only question in his mind asked something he knew nobody had the answer to, but were hoping for it nonetheless.

His father took many sharp turns, to avoid the ruthless men who were trying to catch them. After an hour or so, they left the rugged road and started following a trodden path in the forest. After almost a mile or so, they reached a fenced compound.

Ande, John's father, helped his wife get down from the jeep as John jumped down the backside, and ran over to open the fence gate. Holding it open while nervously scanning the area, his parents rushed inside.

The area was dense with tall pine and birch trees growing all around the fence. Right in the middle was a two-storied building. Ande led his family in; they entered a wide hallway filled with various kinds of computers and knives and automatic weapons.

His father told them they were supposed to wait there for some time until his friend came to rescue them. They were too tired after the stressful journey and sat down on the old sofa kept in the room. And while sitting there, John's father told him the whole story behind their escape.

John's grandfather was a successful Dutchman from the Netherlands. His Dad, Ande Watts, was a loved child who had the liberty to avail all luxuries of life. Money had never

4

been a problem for them as John's grandparents owned several jewelry stores.

It was obvious after his parents' death Ande Watts would inherit the business empire and ultimately John would own the multi-million-dollar family business, but life had some other plans for them.

The day John's grandfather died; his wicked uncle started claiming for his share in the business. He was from the previous wife of his grandfather and was a pureblooded Dutchman. He had contacts with the people in the military. People who did contract work and killing was their daily job. He warned Ande if he didn't accept his demands, the whole family would be killed.

To save his family from his savage brother, he had to flee across the rough terrain as his half-brother hunted for them like a wild animal. Suddenly they heard the sounds of the blade of a chopper, they all rushed to the rooftop, the flying transport was waiting for them. Hours later John awoke landing in lovely Montana to start a new life.

A loud knock at the door brought John back to the room. "Why did you join the military?" Dr. Burke subtly repeated his question. John took a short breath and deeply spoke, "I joined because my father wanted me to."

"Are you sure this was the reason?"

The doctor didn't seem to be convinced. John knew the doctor would keep on asking him until he would be connected to the right answer. This was his job and he was being paid a handsome amount to do it.

At the back of his mind, John always knew he joined the agency for wrong reasons. He always followed his father's instructions and obeyed whatever he wanted him to do.

In fact, he framed his life in however his father wanted him to become. If it were his wish, he would have opted for a more peaceful life filled with the freedom to express genuine love.

However, a person like him who was so much tuned into himself dealt with all problems head-on and rarely expressed emotion, but this year things were entirely different. Being a member of an intelligence agency meant no peace.

Eyes and ears were everywhere. There were people watching the people that watched him. There were people reporting on the people that reported on him. It was like a path that spiraled and spun unto itself. No matter where you went it always led to the same place, to him, watching and waiting for anything unusual to happen. The Agency always protected their investment and John held thousands of national secrets buried in his heart.

For the doctor, he proved to be a tough case, but hopeful. Each time a different aspect of his personality was exposed, Dr. Burke found a puzzle piece of normalcy.

"I joined the Agency because I wanted to carry on my family legacy. My grandfather was the one who decided what was best for my father and my father's successes throughout his life proved my grandfather was not wrong.

So, when it was for me, my father's words and decisions were most important. Joining the military and then the Agency, both these decisions added honor to my family." This time John gave a detailed reply, hoping the doctor wouldn't probe him anymore. Dr. Burke was about to respond, when his cell phone rung. "Excuse me John, I must answer this call, it's my ill father."

John was getting uneasy now and left the chair. "I think it's enough for today doctor, see you in the next session," he said and left the room.

The debriefing session ended there. It had become a routine for a few months now, after returning from any mission, John had an intense session with Dr. Burke and this time the situation was extreme. His mission didn't go the way the Agency and he expected it to be.

Dr. Burke's room was in the small building of the Agency's base hospital. It was entirely built to provide immediate physical and mental medical help to soldiers. While walking back to his apartment, John again started to have flashbacks.

John was fifteen when they reached Montana. So, from a life full of love and rich privilege, where everyone felt loved and bonded with each other, all suddenly turned into darkness and their millions of dollars inheritance was at stake.

Although John was new to the State of Montana, he became popular soon for his cool accent and sexy looks. All the teenage girls wanted to capture his attention because they loved his manly voice with his Dutchman accent and his athletic body.

Time went on and John completed high school. His father was still young and ambitious, so he again established a good business in Montana through his experience and the help of some sincere friends. John wanted to help him to grow the family business, but his dad had other plans for him.

The cruel picture life had displayed for the family, made Ande implement better plans for his son. He wanted John to be powerful and strong enough to protect himself and his own family one-day. At the back of his mind, he feared his half-brother would make all possible attempts to get rid of the last heir of the family, John.

But while doing so, he shattered John's dreams and plans about life. John could never forget how his father prepared him for his military enrollment. He knew his son had to pass a tough physical fitness test before joining, so he stood by his side and guided him through. He made sure his son ran at least five miles a day to build his stamina, take out enough pushups and practice sit ups daily to strengthen his muscles.

Onward, John was on active duty for 25 years when his father died. He fought many unforgettable wars during that time. One of the most difficult one was the Asia Mission. That was right at the start of his career. Like all the other soldiers of his military battalion, John expected it to be a mission full of thrill.

The young troops thought they would be landing on beautiful yellow beaches, offering adventure and sexy curvy women but the reality was different. His battalion was deployed there until the war ended. On his return, his father reminded him he must strive to join the Agency, as he always wanted to see him there.

His professional competence and expertise paved his way to reach his goal and after serving many years he became attached to the most secret elite world Agency. Sadly, his father did not live to celebrate his son's triumph and to witness his wishes being fulfilled because of his extraordinary capabilities.

John soon became an integral part of the Agency. He could design innovative, non-conventional weapons and computer programs. On each achievement, he received felicitations from people around him and he missed his father a lot at that time.

Despite all those successes, there was a painful feeling deep down inside him. It was an unbearable feeling of loneliness. Of despair and dread. He could not escape the feeling that he had spent his life accomplishing someone else's dream. He had always been the man his father wanted, but never the person he wanted himself to be. He had found many ways to solve problems and create weapons that would dazzle even the experts, but he himself was a puzzle. His life didn't go the way he wanted. John had to stop at this point traveling down the memory lane as he had reached his apartment.

He entered the front door and locked it behind him. Then he went to the kitchen to grab a beer. While sitting on the sofa, he sipped his beer and opened his phone gallery. Being a part of such a secret agency, his successes were never known to the public.

People could never realize what sacrifices these unsung soldiers had given for them and had saved them from disasters. So, many agents would collect memories of their achievements in different forms. John gathered those in the form of a massive collection of photos, each one had a very special memory attached to it.

Flipping through the pictures freshened up his mind. Some brought smiles on his face and some made him cry for the loss. These were the glimpses of his golden past, jewels he collected, getting badly hurt at times but still celebrating his achievements.

One of the fondest memories lied in the screenshot, which was the image of the news headline of CNN. The tagline at the bottom was *"A powerful bomb was defused in the capital city saving the life of hundreds of civilians and military personnel.*" John remembered how he put his life in danger while doing that. He received felicitations within the department but not even his mother knew her son's heroic act had saved humanity from disaster. He found solace in the fact that his actions had real, positive consequences, even if he received no fanfare from them.

There was a family picture taken in the backyard of their house in Montana when John was leaving for his military training. His father's face was gleaming with pride, and mom was smiling but she had tears in her eyes. It was difficult to send her only son away from home but the honor and safety of the family demanded that sacrifice.

Then there was a picture of John with his colleagues at a military base in the Middle East. The base was under cyber-attack and no one was able to resolve the problem. Opponents had hacked all the accounts with secret information and they couldn't be reached by any means.

John was a genius at programing, recovering hacked accounts and reopening the secured coded data. He had masterfully crafted a cipher by examining the data patterns themselves. It was something that you could only do if you had a knack for it.

It was indeed a great honor for him when he was called thousands of miles away from his posted base to help find a solution to that issue. In that picture, he was being awarded a shield for his services.

On all those occasions, John missed his father a lot. He thought it was actually his ideal life, which his son is living. His phone gallery was filled with such memories of a man with an exceptional IQ and God gifted qualities that performed extraordinary tasks in and off the field.

John's parents were not religious. They never attended church worship for Sunday service or said a prayer before a meal. But many incidents in his life connected him to God and his faith in God became more and more strong. The first one being how he was saved from his cruel uncle. Then many times during his missions, he witnessed events that made him realize he was sent for some special purpose.

He developed faith working in and out of the field. He recalled a sea mission when he flipped and found his picture smiling and standing in front of the battleship. The ship completely perished after the missile attack and all soldiers on it were killed except John and his best friend Philip.

They jumped in the sea from the burning ship, swam

almost a mile in the freezing cold water and reached the nearest shore. John's life was full of such miracles where it seemed someone was protecting him otherwise; he would have died.

The last picture in the gallery was of John with Philip. It was taken just a day before his last mission ended. They were in combat on a secret mission. He wasn't able to come out of the trauma it had caused him. It cost the life of his best friend Philip.

The enemy used the device designed by John to kill Philip. It was a lethal weapon, and Philip was gone within no time. He was shot from the back. The bullet hit him between his shoulders, and he fell into John's arms. His body began to diffuse and within seconds there was nothing left but a black spot on the ground. Dust was all that remained of his dear friend. John watched with fear, frozen in horror, as he couldn't believe what he saw really happened.

And at that moment, while sitting in his own apartment he buried his head in his knees and mourned for the loss of his dear friend.

CHAPTER TWO

The Hunt

A fter a drunken restless night, John got the text for the next mission. Africa!

"What the…" he said. "Ahhh, Africa!" Shouting to himself with slurred speech singing the chorus line of the Lion King … he stumbles onto his bed and quickly goes to sleep just before sunrise.

Sobering up hours later, he wanted to meet with Dr. Burke before his flight. His mental condition wasn't that stable and he was in dire need of talking his heart out to someone. But at the same time, he thought if the doctor was the right person for doing so. "Nah," he said, and again in German, "Nein!" Thinking aloud, "They won't catch me slipping up." Being an employee of the Agency, under emotional stress and after several cases of beer, John might have said something, which could go against him in the future.

He smiles in the mirror with a shaved face. Emotionally sick, it was difficult to return at that time, as his best buddy was not accompanying him. There were so many missions they accomplished together, they celebrated their successes and mourned their failures. Many times, they were caught in danger and helped one another to get out of it. But that time, Philip wouldn't be there to greet him with a gleaming face when he reached the African base.

On reaching the base, he was given loads of assignments to work on which was good for him. Most of the time he was too busy with his work and his mind was completely shut off from the painful memories. But at night, when he lay in his bed, he couldn't stop himself from recalling the brutal memories of Philip's murder.

After almost a weeklong hectic work routine, he managed to spare some time for himself. He went to the gym for exercise and cardio workouts.

With his headphones in his ears, he listened to a mixed genre of songs. The words from *Looking for Her* took him to a daydream state of mind. His body was working out, but his mind and his heart was in pain. The words pierced his soul. It was his story on looking for genuine love and having internal peace. Singing, "all I want and all I need … is you for me."

Getting teary-eyed, John changed the station and stopped at *Eyes All Over*. The song touched his heart and he started living in it. He left it there because in his life he always felt somebody was watching him. Soon ending his heavy weight-lifting, he sat on the edge of the bench, closed his eyes, and inwardly talked to God, "I am so ready to retire God. Lord, bless me with internal peace. Father, send me the woman you have for me. I am ready for a simple life."

He was satisfied, thinking that he would be retiring soon. It would be his last mission as he had already informed higher authorities; he doesn't want to work for the Agency anymore. He wanted to live a normal peaceful life. It was time he must have his own family. Being a strong-headed person, he was always clear about his goals and what he wanted from life.

John's parents raised him with love and affection under their supervision. His parent's marriage was built on genuine love, respect, honesty, commitment and submission. To John, listening to his parents always held a priority, always, even if what they said didn't always make sense. He had learned long past that he was supposed to listen more than speak up.

This became the building blocks for their loving family. His father was his best buddy. He honored each and every word of his father and which is why he first joined the military and then the Agency.

He never questioned his father on his decisions, as he knew he owed him a lot. He desired the same life for his only son but unfortunately; he wasn't able to develop the same relationship as he shared with his father.

His son Charles was ten years old but John wasn't able to raise him in a normal household. At his son's birth, his girlfriend, who was his son's mom, became her true self. Everything about her was phony.

She had some bigger plans for her life that didn't include John. In utter disappointment, John had to leave his son with his mother; his military job and then Agency assignments did not allow him to raise his son. Later the little fellow was sent to boarding school as John's mother fell ill.

Charles rarely had a chance for good quality time with his dad. Now, when John did visit, it was always the most memorable vacation Charles would have. By the time Charles was ten, he had already traveled to Australia, Singapore, Europe, Greece, and Dubai.

Love and quality time cannot be replaced with travel and materialistic things. So, John desperately wanted Charles's life to change. He so desired to build a strong father-son relationship like he and his dad had. Just before manhood, ten was a good age to get his mini-me from boarding school.

Now on the treadmill, his brain was also working at the same speed. He was trying to counsel himself. He was looking for a true, legit companion who accepted him with all his flaws and would love him with her whole heart. For months he was planning his life after retirement and how he could find a perfect match for himself.

Being a sexy, attractive man, women were always drawn to him but he was very fair in his relationships. If he had a woman in his life, he would remain hers with heart and soul. He didn't like to cheat or betray anyone. But unfortunately, women always came to him attracted by his military status at its peak.

His son Charles's mother was the same, she came to him for the wrong reasons and she was not the person she claimed to be. That bitter experience made John overly cautious, for years he wasn't able to decide whether he should enter into another relationship or not.

He had some other fears too regarding his personal life. His job demanded full devotion and he had to work continuously never being in the same place for too long.

What if he would not able to spare time for his family and couldn't give them true love?

He also thought he could be judgmental about his new companion and might view her in the light of his previous bad experiences. Maybe he'd not be sincere with her. But things were different now. He had decided to retire, to be a loving husband one day and a devoted father. His family would be his mission!

Choosing an ideal life partner was a challenge for him. He had many female colleagues working with him and some of them were good but John wasn't interested in marrying a soldier. With so many tragic memories, he wanted to leave the military behind. He tried military women in the past, but due to the same lifestyle and military stories, in his thirties, he had already opted for civilian women.

Once he had a girlfriend, before Charles' mom, she was his colleague. They shared such a beautiful relationship. She became pregnant and didn't want to raise the child, as her profession didn't give her the liberty to do so. John asked her to leave the job but she wanted to continue.

So, she secretly aborted the child and left him for what she thought was a better life. Years later, John coincidentally saw Sara at a local grocery market. He had accidentally bumped into a woman as he turned off aisle five. He knocked the shopping basket on the floor. As he gathered her things, he noticed a pregnancy test and then gazed up, to his surprise, it was Sara.

Sara was pleasantly excited to see John. They chatted for a bit. She was now married to a much older man, a retired Commander, and desperately tried to get pregnant. The abortion she had of her and John's child scarred her reproductive system making it extremely challenging to naturally conceive. They ended the conversation with a hug. John then casually walked away feeling a sense of closure that she'd be a mom someday soon.

Months back, Philip advised him he should try dating apps to help him find the right match. Before following his advice, John contemplated if he should join the dating site or not. It seemed to be quite a sensible idea so he placed his profile on "ZoZo Match."

There he talked to several women but they were all the same typical women; aiming straight for the bed, calculating what they could earn from John, and weighing his position in society. His job demanded secrecy so he didn't divulge the true nature of his job, but generalized it by stating he worked as an engineer for the military.

Unfortunately, most of the women online came with some emotional baggage from their previous relationships. Many times, he had to ensure again and again his sincerity in the connection. It was hilarious! The women he'd just met online talked to him in a way that looked like they blamed him for the failure of their previous relationships. These women wanted a good man, but they were too wounded by past men to completely trust a new man.

Some men are not as emotional. But because women are mentally and emotionally more in tune than men, some needed assurance from him again and again. In their thought process, John was too good to be true. Then others who were interested in his money, questioned him about his financial stability, and probed about his job nature. One woman even asked if he could pay her past-due utility bills.

Bored and tired of the same problematic women, John did not think he would find a genuine life partner. On day seven, he was about to cancel his subscription, when he came across Lisa's profile. The tagline of her profile attracted him. It said, "Did you read my profile?" It was not like other profiles with pictures to attract men sexually or stimulate their feelings. Her profile felt inwardly different to him.

Lisa was not the average size 10 John was used to. She was curvier in all the right places. So, he read it. It was not an ordinary profile with some short introductory paragraph, then a few pictures or talking about mindless things. It was more in-depth, more like a book of her life. John could easily find the connections with what she wrote about herself.

Lisa was new to the online industry. Her sister introduced her to this world. She was a wholesome, transparent person. She wrote what she wanted in her partner. She had some harsh experiences in life with men. This time she was very clear about what she wanted her partner to be like.

Talking about her faith in God she wrote she loved God and was looking for a God-fearing person to spend her life with. A person with whom she could have open conversations, one who was different from others, liked to travel, and was fun-loving; a person that could love God and still drink a beer while mudding. She wanted someone who was not too religious that he forgot he was once a sinner.

John felt connected to her and sent the first chat. He was flushed typing the first line, "Hello Lisa. I read your profile. I like every word. Can you talk now?" His mind was racing. She wasn't like others who acted as if they were for sale and wanted to achieve everything and anything physically and materialistically at any cost. Lisa was advertising herself to have a life partner with whom she would have a true spiritual dialogue and could find that instinctive connection. A connection where words are felt more than said.

While chatting with her, John simply said he loved her profile, he didn't comment on how pretty or sexy she looked in her pictures. He wasn't dwelling on her beauty but admired her written words. He said he liked the way she explained herself in her profile.

Lisa was selective and rarely replied to people, on the other hand, John continued with one-sided chatting. While scrolling through the messages she stopped at his profile. John showed an inclination toward her. That was the one, which she ignored and had thrown on before, but this time she stopped at his picture and decided to give it a second thought after reading his messages and reading his profile. "Who is this man?" she thought to herself. Intuitively, she felt some special feeling from inside signaling her to give John a chance.

Lisa responded to him, as he was online at the same time. She told John she also liked his profile and then asked some questions about him, his family, and his life. There was a picture of John with his son, Lisa was quite curious about it and discussed his relationship with his son. Then there was another picture in which John was holding a gun in his hand, not in military gear but as if he was going hunting. Lisa had some sense of identifying weapons; she asked John whether he was in the military. John had to lie; he couldn't reveal his identity. So, he said he was, but downplayed his response to a typical engineering job.

To John, Lisa was appealing in many different ways. She never questioned John about his finances because she was looking for a pure relationship. She interrogated a lot, wanting to ensure he wasn't a scam as she was aware there were a lot of scammers online. Once she experienced the same, a man said he was in the military but then she discovered he lied to her.

And then John had the urge to talk to her. He asked her if he could call her. Lisa responded positively. It took several minutes to connect the call. Lisa sat patiently for ten minutes, and then her cell phone rung. John said, "Hi" in a smiling voice and Lisa couldn't help but respond with the same vigor and a smiling tone. Soon they were talking and laughing with one another. They connected so well.

It didn't look like they were talking for the first time. They felt a very strong bond between them, hearing one another's voices sent a sparkling signal through their nerves. Lisa could feel a positive energy emitting from John's voice, which was sending a satisfying sensation through her body.

Hours into the nonstop conversation, they talked to one another openly, discussing their interests, sharing experiences, and common interest. She could hear her mind already telling her he may be the one she had been praying for. John also didn't hold back his thoughts. He told her openly what he wanted in his life partner but didn't mention his job details and also refrained from sharing his plan of retirement for a devoted family life. He thought that was too early in their connection.

They were so engrossed in the conversation that John couldn't hear even the sirens going off on the base.

When he first arrived at the base, he was informed how peaceful it was there. Aside from peacekeeping political matters, his focus was to improve and develop advanced weapons. He had no reason to be on alert.

Suddenly Lisa seemed to be alarmed by the sounds of sirens. She asked John if everything was fine at his end. John was shocked, at how careless he could be. He didn't want Lisa to know his identity and at the same time, he was giving her a situation to be curious about. He was so happily involved in the conversation that he couldn't hear the choppers flying all around and helicopters landing on the roof. He hung up saying he would talk later.

He ran back to the command center. The base was under cyber-attack; rebels were trying to enter the base premises too. In the main hall, all soldiers were lined up listening to the Commander. John hurriedly took his weapons and joined the group. The Commander was briefing his soldiers about the attack of rebels and how important it was to defend the base. A successful attack by the enemy would mean all secret data and classified information would be at their disposal. They had to defend it at any cost or they would be ruined.

At the same moment, Lisa was sitting in her home, smiling to herself, lost in the mesmerizing conversation she had with John. "Oh Lord is this him! She closed her eyes and fell asleep.

CHAPTER THREE

Lisa McDaniel

While she slept, she dreamed heavily about John. She was inquisitive about him; her brain was giving positive vibes to her. She wanted to find out more about him, who he was, what he does, and so on. She was buried in her dreams until a thud on the door woke her from her slumber. "Who could it be?" she thought to herself as she peeped through the eyehole. And on seeing the visitors outside she couldn't help but shout in great excitement, "Well! Well! Who do we have here now?"

She hugged her sisters tightly as they entered her home. "Busy Bee Lisa, where you have been for the last so many days, we were worried," Rachel asked her. "I dropped messages for you but you didn't reply!" Marwella too bombarded her this time with her neck twisting while rolling her eyes, Lisa laughed aloud and once again wrapped her arms around them. She was missing her sisters immensely but wasn't able to talk to them for the last several days. She had been too busy with her business deals. Being a successful real estate entrepreneur wasn't easy. It had taken her years of hard work to establish a good position in the market as a real estate investor and developer.

It was so refreshing to connect with her sisters after a big gap. Sitting there while sipping wine, they recalled how crazy they had been in their teen years. They had a handful of friends who loved to do the same wild activities together. Many times, they planned blind dates in which one would pretend to be the other sister.

And then they recalled watching scary movies and then playing pranks on each other seeing who got scared the worst. Lisa was warned twice at high school, as she loved to pop lock dance on the lunchroom tables. There were so many things to remember and enjoy together. "Hey Lisa, did you find anyone of your type on ZoZo Match?" Marwella asked her. She was the queen of social media in the family and advised everyone to find solutions to their love life problems on ZoZo Match.

And at that moment Lisa shared with them how excited she had been after finding John online. She told them everything about him and also her intuitions, how she was feeling attracted towards him. "I have faith in God. The way he talks left me intrigued. The intellectual conversation was so stimulating.

It's good to finally have a decent conversation with a man where there is no debating. In fact, I never had such a strong feeling for anyone in my life before. Really, for me, to know I can feel so deeply over a mere conversation is shocking."

This left her sisters curious. They wanted to find out more about John before Lisa moved forward with him. "I believe in whatever you said sistah girl but be careful this time. You had already suffered a lot before.

Rachel was worried; "Men are cunning and love to drive us crazy when they assume they have us for keeps." Lisa knew she was right in her fears. She had sheltered herself from the dating scene and became very cautious. Being a successful businesswoman was not easy when dealing with wealthy people and social media. So, she wasn't interested in the fantasy world of social media much.

She had clients all over everywhere and carried a good reputation. An incorrect or inconsiderate post would have been damaging. Envious people lurk all around waiting to spread lies and steal your joy. And, her brothers were already known for their wild side. So, she didn't want others to have the chance to think negatively about her being involved with men on social dating sites.

Thankful her Mr. Right could be John, she escaped the conversation thinking to call him. She wanted to give him a chance in her life. Her previous experiences were not really good with men and triggered negative feelings in her for the opposite sex.

Desiring to contact John felt good and was a positive change. Her walls were starting to crack and not because of his sexy and strong personality but because of her intuition, which was compelling her to move forward.

Sipping her wine, as her thoughts raced about, her mind was always in many places. The three sisters shared a very strong bond. Rachel was the eldest among the siblings, and she always took care of them like a mother. Lisa always thought she had been very lucky to have a loving and caring family. Marwella was two years younger than Lisa so Lisa was the middle child.

In hope of a prosperous future in the automotive industry, their parents moved to Detroit from the South in the early 70s. Both of them were active civil rights activists during the General Motors labor movement. Known for their bold stance and charismatic personalities, they held important positions in the movement. Unfortunately, when Lisa was five years old and Marwella only two, a ruthless gang member killed their mom. Other activists assumed the murderers were hired hands assigned to warn their father to quit the movement if he wanted his daughters to be safe.

Rachel was ten at that time, a much more responsible and grown-up girl for her age. She told her sisters; her mom reminded her since her tender years she had to take care of her sisters. For his family, their father had to make some major decisions. He left Michigan and moved to Georgia where he became a Mega Pastor at a popular church. Lisa was ten at that time. Later her father decided to get married to a woman who was divorced and had two twin sons. She was twelve and her twin stepbrothers were fourteen years old when their families blended.

The twins introduced her to a new picture of life as they lived on the wild side. They were smart young boys who later grew into charismatic businessmen – gentle when you know them, but ruthless to outsiders. That was appealing to her. She always enjoyed hanging with them and they were also too kind to her and never stopped her. They had relations with all the wrong people and by the age of thirteen, Lisa was aware of all the dark sides of the wild world.

Reminiscing, the other guy with whom she loved to hang out was her high school boyfriend, Tony. He was a handsome sixteen-year-old. Tony was the popular teen quarterback with girls racing after him. But he told Lisa he only wanted to be with her.

She was thirteen when Tony took her to his home on Sunday after Church service. His mom was in the kitchen fixing Sunday dinner while chatting with her sisters in the living room. Tony briefly introduced Lisa to his aunts before heading to his bedroom to hang out.

The door closed as his mom shouted dinner would be ready in an hour. They were on the couch kissing. Then he lured her to his bed. She was nervous and unsure of the sexual tension. She thought it was an innocent make-out moment, but the situation turned dark when Tony passionately kissed her causing her to lie back on the bed.

His face became a pressing weight. Every muscle in his body was fired up against her small frame. He positioned himself on top of her and unzipped his pants. She told him she was not ready for sex, and, he knew she was still a virgin. He tried to quiet her by saying it will be ok. He was not going to penetrate her. He said it would be innocent and the grinding would feel good.

Lisa was caught up in the moment and continued on. They

continued kissing. Then Tony got more intense and pulled her skirt up. Lisa, feeling uneasy, wanted no part of it. Her mind went blank thinking how could he rape her. I am so supposed to be married first.

She told Tony to stop and that excited him more, he then put his hand over her mouth while trying to pull out his penis from his pants. He quickly tried to insert himself in Lisa, but Tony was too big for her, the pain felt awful. She moved her head trying to wiggle free, and then she bit his hand and murmured for him to stop.

He pressed his hand down harder. She bit him again and muffled I am going to tell your mom, who was in the next room. He then stopped the penetration and gently kissed her trying to calm her down. He was so worked up he forgot they were not alone. Lisa sat up from the bed.

Shaking, she pulled down her skirt and slowly stood by the couch. She could not sit down because of the pain. She told him she wanted to go home. She felt dirty as sweat and blood drizzled down her legs. As he gave her a shirt to wipe off with, she thought how could she have let herself get into a situation like that? She thought how could Tony rape me. No means No! It does not matter how it starts; Stop means Stop! She calmed herself down not wanting anyone to know.

Shame and self-blame took over her mind.

Tony blamed it on him being experienced and wanting her so badly. That he could not control himself because she was so beautiful. Basically, he apologized to avoid getting in trouble while telling her it was her fault because she was so beautiful. Tony's mom soon shouted, "yawl come on out, the banana pudding is ready." Wiping her face and fixing her skirt, it was showtime. Lisa walked out with a phony smile as Tony tightly held her hand.

Skipping the banana pudding tasting, he escorted Lisa outside to call her sister. Soon after, Rachel picked her up from Tony's house. Rachel sensed the sadness and pain, but Lisa was too ashamed and scared to share it with anyone. She had a unique way of surpassing trauma believing God would handle those who hurt her. Her belief became reality when she heard Tony died of a heart attack in his thirties.

By the next memory, her face was frowning. Marwella thought it was about her crazy story of eating chocolate ants, but it was another bad relationship experience. Her twin brothers were in their twenties and Lisa was two years younger than them. One got injured while playing pro basketball overseas and the other took his degree in business studies from DeVry University.

They returned home and opened a popular nightclub. Those were exciting times for the girls and they were overwhelmed by that crazy lifestyle. The nightclub was exotic, somewhat unique for its type. There were indoor waterfalls where women with barely any clothing danced in cages. Men came, drank, chose partners, and then went to private meeting rooms for their private affairs and wrongful business dealings.

Whatever the dark side of that lifestyle wanted, the brothers welcomed and earned a lot from it. They told their sisters there wasn't anything wrong there. The money was sweet like honey. Gradually the three sisters too became immune to that life and started meeting people. The club life was their schoolmaster offering free lessons in every aspect of fun sinfulness. All of their dad's sermons were internally buried.

Lisa later met Larry at the age of twenty there. They had a long relationship for several years. She thought they would marry. She even dreamt of having a child with Larry. But that was not her child. Apparently, he had gotten another woman pregnant.

Their relationship was rocky as Lisa always wavered between enjoying worldly pleasures versus serving God faithfully. She let sex bind her to Larry. The final breaking point of their relationship ended when he brutally raped her at age twenty-seven.

She knew he was addicted to pornography. They both watched and learned. It was fun in the beginning. However, he became consumed. What he saw, he wanted. She did not care to have anal sex. It was unclean to her. But porn videos gave the illusion it was clean and easy to do.

On that horrible day, they initially enjoyed each other. In his bedroom room, he always kept a container of sex lubricant on the nightstand. It helped, as his penis was above average. Lisa was lying on her stomach booty-but naked watching TV. They had just finished round two of sex.

Larry lubed up, nothing abnormal at first. He started kissing her neck and rubbing her erogenous areas. He gets in position and penetrated her vaginally, and then suddenly he took out his penis and forced himself in her anally. It was the most uncomfortable and hurtful experience. She remained lying on her stomach. He pressed her arms down above her head and stretched out his 6' 2" body on top of her backside.

There was nothing she could do but scream. His breath was hot as warm sweat dripped from his face onto her left ear as he deeply said, "To relax, it won't be long. Dam, you feel so good. Don't fight me." Again, she screamed for him to stop. His penis slipped out. She thought he was stopping, but she was wrong. He forced himself inside her again.

Unable to move, she screamed louder as the weight of his 230-pound body made the second penetration worse with less lubricant. To quieter her, he reached for a pillow as he continued to thrust and placed it over her head. Now, she could not breathe.

She did not want to die that way. Smothered by a pillow with him thrusting inside her anus was too much to endure. She tried to lift his hands, but she was not strong enough.

He knew she was struggling. Not wanting to kill her, he slightly removed the pressure of the pillow and allowed her to turn her head to the side to quickly breathe. As she looked toward the slender rectangular bedroom window, she saw someone approaching his apartment, and so did Larry. He started going faster to ejaculate.

He finished his dirty rape happy he accomplished getting what he wanted. Sliding his penis out of her open anus, he tapped her booty with his hand and went to the bathroom as if nothing brutal happened. She remained on her stomach afraid to move.

Her anus felt wide open, she felt sensations of pain, constipation, and diarrhea. She lay there paralyzed in fear. Not wanting to face the sick reality of the crime he just committed, he tells her to get up, that his friend was outside. She turned on her side and he grabbed her hand to pull her off the bed. Her lower body was weak and she was unable to stand without trembling.

To brace herself from falling to the floor, she had to lean on his chest wrapping her hands around his waist for stability. Blind to the crime he committed, he thought she was showing affection and kissed her on the forehead as if she enjoyed it.

He helped her to the bathroom and handed her a black washcloth. The water ran with her hovering against the sink. She slowly washed over her sore anus, put on her clothes, and wobbled to the front room to leave. She could not look at him anymore. No more kind words or sexual gestures.

The rocky relationship was now a mudslide. After having such a strong trusting sexual relationship for years, it was difficult for her to absorb. How could a man whom she believed she knew so well for seven years could disgrace and brutalize her and possibly have suffocated her? Shamed again she felt. Though older, she never reported the crime, but again believed God would handle it. Years later, after he apologized, Larry became diabetic and loss his vision.

At a new start in life, Lisa had a new attitude. Her father urged her to return to the Church, repent of her sins, and start dating a Christian man. This time she chose a mature Christian partner with a strong financial position. Her husband was a very successful man. However, his love was conditional.

He loved and cherished her when she was not challenging. She was okay with allowing him to lead but wanted the same respect and submission in return. However, his respect for her was short-lived. She was tired of staying at home and not contributing to their life.

She wanted money to invest in her business ventures. But her husband was always opposed to all of her bright ideas. He had no faith in her never trusting her ingeniousness. He felt it was the man's role to make risky financial decisions since he had a greater responsibility to be the provider.

But he failed to realize they were an equal partnership. That whatever financial gains occurred in the marriage belonged to Lisa as well. He failed to love his wife as he loved himself. Unfortunately, he was a player that forced his teammate to the bench. On the sidelines, he told her he wanted a family with a wife similar to sitcoms in the 1950s.

Tired of sexually charged and wounded men, Lisa gave in. Her life was dormant and she developed low self-esteem. Her husband overshadowed her in all aspects and never cared to realize she also had her own dreams.

Interestingly, people envied her. They thought she was living an ideal life with a flawless perfect Christian man, so caring with rich finances. To them, he was the complete package a woman could wish for but for Lisa, it was a challenging relationship.

Being a good wife, she supported him throughout in fulfilling his business dreams but he in return never invested in her. He appeared to be an extremely humble, caring, and faithful life partner for Lisa and kind to all others but in reality, he was self-obsessed.

A few years into their marriage, he started spending many long hours at work. Lisa was married but felt single. He cared less about vital quality time. He felt it was cheaper to keep her, and failed to adore her. But, a nice home and money can only do so much.

He was married to his job giving much of his attention to his employees. Lisa felt emotionally cheated on and her dreams led her to see he physically cheated. So, on finding a better option, Lisa divorced him after tracing his locations on Google. Come to find, he had time to visit an apartment complex near his job. Erica was her name, or maybe Linda or Roxanne. Actually, there were quite a few questionable women.

At the age of thirty-eight, she was divorced. And that was the time her journey of self-discovery took its flight. She regretted having bad relationships and vowed to take a break from men for a while. She needed time to discover herself without any relationship distractions.

Reflecting, she worked so hard to achieve her true potential and there she stood as one of the most successful businesswomen in her city. She was free of bad men and manipulative people in her life, scratching all relationship drama out. She became confident about her choices, knew her value, and could make better decisions for herself.

Coming out of her flashback Lisa glanced at her sisters. "Finally, you snapped back into reality," said Marwella.

Rachel chimed in, "Mmmhmm, this experience is stirred up emotions, huh? Giggling, you truly are momma's mini me." They were inquisitive and wanted to know more. They knew Lisa had strange dreams, which indicated her future. Rachel told her she had inherited that trait from her mother and grandmother. Rachel and her father thought her mother always knew she had less time in the world.

It was strange. One day she felt the urgency to train the girls in household tasks. They were all so young. She trained her eldest daughter in a way that she could handle the family at a very young age. At age 10, Rachel could write checks for bills, wash clothes, iron, cook, and bake.

And the day she died she definitely knew death was coming. Mostly Marwella accompanied their mother when she went out for different errands, but on the day, she was murdered, she left Marwella home with Rachel. Their dad is still haunted by those events, wishing he was more observant and asked more questions. That perhaps, she would have lived if he were more proactive. But, deep down, Rachel believed momma knew her death was certain to happen.

Lisa also had the same spiritual premonitions in her dreams, as Rachel always thought. When Lisa, was seven, she bought Lisa her first dream journal. As a kid, she drew pictures, and now she wrote stories. Rachel with a bottle of wine in one hand walked over to Lisa's bookshelf and grabbed her latest dream book. In one hand, she held it tightly to her chest. Then turns around and walk to the center of their circle. Still holding the dream book close, she then raised the bottle of wine with her right hand, "Cheers to dreaming. Cheers to momma. Cheers to family." By that time, they were completely drunk after drinking seven bottles of wine. With heavy heads, they all fell asleep on the sofas.

Lisa dreamed of herself being on another planet. She saw John there in the wild fighting a war and Lisa witnessing it. It was a long dream. She saw him running, the enemy following him. The enemy surrounded him and then he fell into a ditch. Lisa woke up; she was sweating profusely, and short of breath. "Was I also running with him for his life?"

Rachel and Marwella left the next morning with a promise to meet soon. The following few days were not that busy. The business was slowing down due to COVID. One day after having online meetings with her clients, Lisa had another strange dream. She saw a family, John and herself being a part of it. This was the weirdest dream she ever saw, a very strong sign for her. She started making connections,

John's picture with the military gun, and her dream of him being at war, and now being a family with him. "I need to talk to him, there are many things I want to ask about," she murmured to herself. She couldn't resist the urge to connect to John and messaged him to talk to her.

CHAPTER FOUR

Over Easy

John answers immediately. It seemed he was also waiting for her message. Lisa had a feeling, he sensed to be happy and already involved in the relationship. John was at an undisclosed base in Africa on an assigned mission. At that time, he was free and had the urge to talk to her too.

Lisa asked him to send more photos, she wanted to make sure he was real and life is not again throwing her a dramatic curve ball. She wanted to observe his personality deeply. Sometimes a photo speaks more than the person and she knew her instincts would give her distinct messages about him. The photo he sent portrayed a strong, masculine, and protective man.

And then she magnified the picture, focusing on his deep, hazel, talking eyes. She always thought eyes are a key to one's soul, they show who you are and what you are going through. To Lisa his eyes were like an open book, signaling his mind was running loose like a freight train off-track!

She instantly texted John, "your eyes seem so heavy; they say you have a lot to talk about. I'm here for you if you need me to listen." John, without waiting for a moment, replied,

"Is it a good time to talk," and called her.

He opened up with her and started discussing his life issues. He thought, "I have found the right woman for my life, Oh God, I can't believe I'm talking to her!" While talking, he could feel an intuitive bond, a strong spiritual connection with her. Sometimes our sixth sense signals us when we meet genuine people in our lives, and John could already sense it. They were born to be together. As far as Lisa was concerned, her special spiritual abilities were giving her very strong signals.

She believed in him, in every single word he said about himself and his life. She thought how could he make so much drama in his life? It must be true. Surprisingly, whatever Lisa figured about him after seeing his latest picture, he was proving to be the same genuine person.

Together, with every word shared, they were laying a strong foundation for their future life. He told her many things about his past life experiences and talked a bit about his family too. Then he told her he had to go and would talk to her very soon again. After hanging up, he felt refreshed and recharged for the day ahead. The conversation was like a volt of energy for him, getting him ready for a positive routine ahead.

The next morning, he woke up and found something exciting on his phone. Lisa had sent a morning picture of her natural self, with no makeup, with a pure, bright smile. He couldn't curb his instant urge to talk to her; he wanted to listen to her sweet voice. He dialed her number and on hearing her voice he said in his deep foreign voice, "Hello the world's most beautiful woman, you are my SUNSHINE!"

Lisa was also having the same feeling. All night she thought about him in how well they clicked. They could talk about any aspect of life. For the first time ever, words flowed so easily with a man. Wanting him to see her natural state, she couldn't resist and sent him her picture. She was his sunshine as her beauty was magnified radiating with joy about John.

That day he talked a lot about his family. He told her his dad was his best friend and when he was alive, he never needed anyone else to be his friend. His death left him heartbroken and dejected. It took him several years to rise again. He had always been selective when it came to people.

To the people who were close to him, he was like an open book, and to Lisa, he had the same feeling. She asked him more about his family, his children, and his ex-girlfriend.

John told her he had only one son Charles. Lisa could already sense Charles' mother had not been good to them.

Being in tune with John, she could hear the negative energy in his voice about his ex-fiancé. She sensed deceptive negative energy about her personality. John admitted he was caught up in her physical appearance when they first met. "She was beautiful, but not a natural beauty like you Lisa," John said. There was always an uncomfortable feeling about Maria.

John revealed she was a trap laid for him. He met her on a mission and they became close to one another with each passing day. The relationship continued for many years. When she was pregnant with Charles, he brought her home to live with his parents. Mostly John was off on different missions and she was there at home befriending his parents, especially his mother.

She told John he shouldn't worry about home life and to work with full devotion; she was there to take care of their family home and also the family business. To gain his family's support she told them what miserable life she led before meeting John. She ran away from her foster family, as they were verbally and physically abusive. Unfortunately, his parents could not obtain a background check, as Maria did not have a criminal record on file. John's parents only knew what Maria divulged.

She presented the ideal picture of a sweet woman who overcame many hardships. She was a self-made person very knowledgeable and willing to help. All this was a part of the game she was playing with the family. The extended truth after she ran away is she met a new family.

Almost a year after running away, a notorious Columbian gang then became her everything. One of the lead gang members found her homeless living in an abandoned building. He was amazed at how a fifth grader could survive in the streets for so long without protection.

Viewing how intelligent she was, he trained her to be a deceptive force. She could manipulate anyone. Her criminal activities required her to be trustworthy and manipulative. Being so manipulative spawned the best pathological liar known in the streets who always kept her story straight. Half the time she didn't know who she was.

Sometimes she regretted being part of it. She started loving John truly but she knew the gang wouldn't let her leave. She was raised by the best street criminals in South America, and she knew too many of their secrets. No matter how she felt toward John, she belonged to the gang for life, and the reality was cruel.

She was glued to John for his financial status. A woman like her wouldn't miss a chance to extract benefits from several jewelry stores John's father operated. She loved John but hated the strong family ties, which bound them together. She thought they were too empowering, affecting her personal life and her goals and she couldn't penetrate them no matter how hard she tried to do so.

John's father was an experienced man. After all, he was running a big business for years and had the sense of identifying real and fake people. He could figure out something was going in the wrong direction but needed to confirm it further. His mother was a simple housewife though. She couldn't identify the cunningness in that lady's nature and always thought positively about her. Maria was like a daughter to John's mom.

She lived with them for three years. Then chaos soon reached their home life and his child was also being neglected whereas John's mom spent most days caring for Charles alone. Greed was Maria's downfall. She started intervening in business issues. By the time her fraud was revealed in the audit report, she stole nearly two million dollars. With the help of her gang, she created a fake ID for operating John's personal bank account, and handled the company's accounts payable. She embezzled most of the money in offshore accounts.

At that moment, while talking to Lisa John's voice was full of pain and agony and Lisa could feel it while sitting miles away from him. He went on to say how all this left his father dejected. He was very furious and wanted to send Charles' mother to prison but John pleaded with him not to do so.

Going to the police meant other issues would arise, mainly the custody of his son. He didn't want the mother to take the child away; he knew his son's life would be ruined. So, he made a deal and spared her at the cost of acquiring his son's custody. Standing before a judge without a tear in sight, she relinquished her parental rights over to John's mom.

According to the last news, she settled in New York. It took years for John to rebuild himself after that betrayal and she was the last woman he had in his life before Lisa arrived. His father wasn't very happy with his decision but his mother supported John's decision to exchange her parental custody for her freedom. After that incident, their family business never flourished again. They were in extreme financial hardship and that left his father heartbroken. His health deteriorated with every passing day. He couldn't manage the stress, he worked so hard to establish the business empire and a lady came and destroyed it in only three years!

Ande died two years later while John was in the Middle East. Unable to break cover, he was devastated not being able to attend the funeral in person. Though his mother tried to comfort him by sending the most picturesque funeral pictures, his journey overseas was gloomy. The desire to light his own lantern for the lake ceremony left a hole in his heart. Lisa could hear John crying, "I miss him so much. I should have been there." Lisa chimed in, "You were where Ande wanted you to be. Remember how he trained with you to prepare you."

John was losing focus. Remembering that day flooded his spirit with unmanageable grief. He went silent on Lisa for a while. Understanding the trauma, she held the phone in silence. However, Lisa was unaware of his flashbacks. At this time, he recalled the best way to honor his dad, which was by staying alive on every mission. Seeing visions of himself showing no mercy for anyone haunted him. He had just slit a man's throat and as the blood dripped from the knife, he snapped back to reality,

"Hey SUNSHINE! Sorry about that. Awe you are so patient and sweet with me. Thank you for you! So where was I?" Lisa changed the subject, "You said, you joined the Agency." John said, being a little disoriented, "Yes, right? After I returned home. I joined the Agency in the same year my dad died. It was the best way to honor him." Lisa interrupted and uplifted his spirits by saying, "You are my manly man. An awesome son! And, I feel Ande is very proud of you." She then sucked the phone dry and sent an air kiss along with several emoji hugs to comfort him. John chuckles and spins around in his chair, I got them all babe." Lisa ends the call wishing him well.

The next day, He sent a photo of Philip to her mentioning "My other precious friend" whom I lost. So, in their next conversation, he talked about his relationship with Philip.

"He has been my best buddy since I came to the States. We met at the airport and somehow became really good friends over the years. He was supposed to go to college and become a commercial pilot but he changed plans and joined the same military branch as me. He stood in the way of a bullet aimed at me in 2003 on our first deployment together overseas. Later on, he died in my arms.

I miss my bestie so much, he's the only one who ever broke through my spirit and reached my heart along with my parents. And now the final person who came close to my heart is you, Lisa, my Sunshine!" He was laying it on heavy; John quoted the bible, "A man who finds a wife finds a good thing." Clear about his goals well aware of what he wanted in life, Lisa was becoming to mean so much to him and he had already started imagining his future life with her.

With Lisa on his mind, everyone could see some sort of smile on his face and the soldiers would tease him. "After losing Philip, and having lost so many past comrades, I distanced myself from strengthening new relations, never smiling or engaging with others. I was afraid of getting close to anyone. The fear of death was always so close. It could snatch your loved ones from you any time."

His family business couldn't flourish again after his father's death as the world was hit by the pandemic. He told Lisa about his military team that had undergone trials for experimenting with the vaccine for COVID. Experiments were being conducted on military officials before passing it down to the civil population. That was no doubt one of the worst phases of his life.

With each passing day, the fear of the unknown was mounting, people were dying in thousands and all were helpless. He had to stay indoors; the pain was unbearable. At times it was difficult to breathe, he was scared, there was no one on his side to take care of him and he thought one day he would die alone on a base and no one would ever know. At last, he survived and came out of that phase stronger.

Then he talked about his military projects. He was too caught up, as his profession demanded a lot of time and effort. He didn't have many friends and couldn't make a bond with people. He had special skills to design weapons, especially bombs. He was the pioneer in introducing many new techniques and designs in weapon making. Lisa already felt proud of herself; such an extraordinary person is going to become her MANLY-MAN in the future.

Everyday their relationship was growing stronger. John felt Lisa was the one he prayed for to be in his life. He didn't know her father was a mega pastor or how much Lisa knew about the Bible, John was caught up in her positivity and would text her very often to share all his feelings and emotions. For Lisa, she could relate all that to herself. Not getting to know her mother past age two was sorrowful, so she understood John's feelings after losing his father and

Philip. He texted her, "Please listen to me, you are a woman of God and he listens to you, I can affirmatively say!" He told her he was like all the other guys earlier, loved to party, and spent time with girls but then his life changed as he developed a strong connection with God after some weird experiences on certain missions.

He could consciously feel the presence of another spirit, perhaps an angel, around him, guiding and guarding in each situation. Once he was shot and fell to the ground lying in his own blood. Every breath he took was excruciatingly painful. Gazing toward heaven, he saw an angel coming toward him. The angel was extremely tall as if a massive cloud was going to sandwich him into the earth. Hovering at first then quickly standing beside John, the angel reached out his hand and as John grabbed the angel's hand, tiny halos surrounded him. He felt a pulsing sensation throughout his body.

Touching the angel, John saw his son crying, saying he wanted his daddy to come home. Not giving up on life, he rolled over and lifted himself up starting with his knees. Then the angel reached out his other hand and John stood on his feet. The angel spoke and said, "Remember your son." John limped 30 miles through the rugged terrain before being seen by his comrades.

Lisa shared the same feelings with him. She shared her family details with him about how her father was called to preach and how her family and home environment changed forever. They experienced the unseen realms of good and evil. For seven days, God protected and transformed her father's thought process.

The Spirit of God was so great in their home that circles of tiny halos floated throughout. They were surprised; the resemblance in their spiritual life stories was striking. That further strengthened their belief in one another. It seemed they were destined to be together.

His days at the base were getting busier. At times he would lose communication for hours with her but as soon as he had time he would text her, "Good day Sunshine, working to bring all surveillance systems and communications back to normal. Not hearing your voice had eaten me up. I didn't get a chance to tell you … I feel on the top of the world when we talk, I miss your voice, babe." Lisa commented, "I miss talking to you as well."

She also vents herself by texting him about her brother's child. How his father and mother wanted him to be a good

Christian student at school but never taught him about God. A child could not easily become what he never saw at home. Her nephew's parents where not Christian role models. They never gave him lessons in kindness and needed lessons themselves. When he saw her message late at night, he texted her while she was asleep.

"They must read the Bible or pray with their kid if they want him to be a good Christian. I often debate and quiz my son when it comes to the word of God. That bond and connection when reading the word and praying together are glorious as a child should be able to rely greatly on his parents spiritually, mentally, physically, emotionally, and financially. Or else they would go and sort their reliability elsewhere. Ultimately, they would end up in a bad and unwanted circle. Everything the parents perceived would come down crashing on their kids. This is my thought for a family.

As a father, I pray and read the words of God with my family. I'm the sort of person who would not overlook the spiritual growth and development of his family. I look forward to being the final, serious man in your life. If you would let me Sunshine, I want to be everything you prayed for in your dream man."

The next morning, Lisa read his text and was in awe of John. She could not find a better name to give him than her FIRST-CLASS MAN, the man strong enough to break through her walls. She called him and as soon as he picked up her call, she said, "Good morning, First-Class, I can imagine you wearing your invisible cape on the base.

Ahhh, you have captured my spirit with this reply. Thank you for every word you wrote, it resonates so well with my soul. I wanted a man for so long like you, as you spiritually describe yourself with your son. You know– talk it and live it. Oh my, how you stated the way a child should rely on his parents is what I too have always believed." John was charged after listening to her voice. He could definitely say it was the most pleasant morning of his life.

"The foundation of any home starts with the spirit of God filling it with those focused on His word," she added. "Ephesians" is one of my favorite books because it talks about the structure of God in the family and the unknown realms we unseeingly wrestle with. Indeed – I too would like to be on a good journey with you. We may never know what is ahead of us, but with God directing our steps, we can accomplish any rocky road together.

We would blissfully magnify the power of true love

together, embracing the spirit of God as God always intended the family unit to be. Life is a journey First-Class, and it can be glorious when the path is paved in the right spirit with the right person. You make happy, John Watts and you ain't even here. Wow, it's going to be something amazingly great when I feel your energy in person."

John replied, "I'm happy, you are happy, that's all I crave for us, happiness, peace, beauty, longevity, abundance, and much more. I'm no longer afraid to say I love you...bcoz I do so." And then John wanted to start making future plans. John told Lisa he wanted them to buy a minimum of 3 acres of land and to have a large home with a pool and garage for the many trucks and vehicles he would buy. "I want a home life retreat where we can relax and be happy with each other all day every day," said John. "I want to know all of your family and for you to be Charles's mom. My future is you. No more military life."

Lisa replied, how could you say this so soon? John replied, "I feel it in my SOUL. We are meant to be, you will see, and soon you will say - I love you too to me, John sends a smile emoji and a kiss, "you're my dream now."

Lisa hadn't opened up yet about her financial status, it had only been fifteen days since they discussed a forever life and she thought she must hold back some things to reveal further. She was very infatuated with John. After they had a conversation about sex, they shared the same desires. This was rare as most people can be sexually unbalanced.

The connection kept burning inside her, and she was learning to love him. John was the ball to her chain. John explained to her how he had his share of women in his life and was looking for a spiritual connection like they had.

Lisa asked him what if she wanted him to wait to have sex until they were married. John didn't hesitate and said yes. He told her he was already in love with her and desired no other woman in his life. So, whatever she wanted to be done, that was done! "I want God's blessings for us, nothing but happiness, peace, and love. I just want to retire, never ever go on another mission, John stressing every syllable. I want you by my side, for Charles to have a mother like you and grow our family's jewelry business in America. This is my dream babe, to create a legacy with you. To have infinite love."

CHAPTER FIVE

Shelled

John was thrilled to find her. He was on a cloud souring high, and already planned much in advance. Before hanging up that evening he told her it was high time they should meet, he wanted to physically feel her presence. Her voice completely shut him from the world; he couldn't hear the sudden desperate alarms ringing around him. The base was under attack. Even Lisa, sitting thousands of miles away could hear the ringing sirens but for the first time ever John was lost in his dreams. "Is everything alright at your end?" John shrugged his body at this question and came back to the present world. He acted calm, "Oh yesssssss, everything's fine, I think it's an ambulance passing by seems there is an emergency at the security checkpoint, we'll talk later Sunshine, let me check," and he hung up.

He rushed to the command center to join his team and learned the situation was extremely critical. Rebels had launched a successful cyber-attack on the base, cutting off vital communication systems, and were then attempting to jam their radar system and other devices. That would mean complete destruction. They were hundreds of miles away from the nearest town. An attack with no outside communication lines would have shattered the secret base where soldiers could become captives for months, maybe years. The Commander briefed his soldiers; the enemy has pulled a fast one on us and had been spying on us as well. They have certain vicious underlying plans. Trust no one; it was up to the soldiers now who had to stop them at any cost.

The base was situated near a mountain surrounded by a deep African jungle all around. The enemy had deep roots not only in the community around them but also it was certain someone within the Agency was working as their double agent, providing them with all the necessary information and the maps of the premises. They were forced to go out and fight on the ground with them, there was no way out, communication lines were already lost and the radar system was at stake. The Commander ordered, "Take your spy dogs, your weapons, and all necessary equipment with you. Hunt for them everywhere, don't leave any stone unturned. Spread in the jungle below, if they are not stopped, we could become helpless out here for years!"

John was upset. He had already resigned, going into the battlefield physically would mean fighting a war, hunting for people, killing them, capturing them as prisoners, and even killing yourself! Who knew who would survive or die! He was desperate to get out of all this and start a new life with his family. Putting on his gear, he fussed and prayed. Every prayer started with freakin war -- protect us all God. Freakin war -- give us victory. Suddenly, he feels a heavy presence overcome him as he humbly said forgive me now and for what we are about to do, Amen!"

They had some special radar-like devices already planted deep in the ground to watch for the dangers in the thick forest down below. Now they were supposed to hunt each and every mountain cave, the nooks, and grooves find out enemy fighters, kill them or conquer them. But before that, they had to dig out a deeply buried device from the ground and shift it to another place. The maneuvering mechanics was delayed, and the ultrasonic radar detection was weak. With night vision goggles, it was not an easy task. As ordered by the Commander, only a handful of soldiers were involved, and John was a part of that team. Using micro-bombs John made, they loosened the ground around the device. They then placed thousands of mechanical mining nano-bots in the opening to expand the hole. As the nano-bot diggers extracted the soil, their mechanical silver coating appeared like tiny crusty white stones. With so many nano-bots together, the soil around them was glittering in the moonlight. It was not a normal piece of ground; it had some hidden treasure in it! Yes, it was full of diamond traces, that was their first thought.

They knew Africa was known for its underground treasures; especially rare stones and this could be one of those. That left the soldiers startled, they were doubtful at first blaming the visuals on the long strenuous day they had. Then one soldier persuaded the others to think that was the reason they were assigned to the secret base in the middle of nowhere. Another soldier did his tribal dance as he shouted, "Fellas! I think we just opened a billion-dollar hole, thank you mother earth!" John shook his head, "it's not our land." A smiling man gently shoved John's shoulder and one jokingly said, "Ahhh nothing is better than that woman who makes you smile." The team leader whistles loudly to gather his crew, enough talk, finish up men, sunrise is hours away."

Soldiers still whispering and imagining their wannabe rich lifestyle finally got focused and finished mounting the radar detector at a better location. John gathered the nano-bots that were covered in diamond dust. The radar picked up a hundred enemy men within a mile of their location. There were two enemies for every soldier to kill. The hunt was extreme. Bullets were rarely used. The soldiers used titanium arrows and advanced tactical knives to rip the enemy apart. It was a bloody massacre. They kept three rebels alive and took them to the base.

The men were tortured until they answered. One rebel, barely able to speak said, "We were protecting the area from the new political regime. You Americans! You protect the wrong side. Spitting up blood, he further said, this land is our land. No new government is going to change that." The rebel's voice faded out."

The second rebel, a tall muscular man, sees the nano-bots in John's container and said, "Greed is the root of all evil?" The Commander walks over to the third rebel and whispers in his ear, then commands the earthy material on the nano-bots be tested. On testing the soil samples, they found out there was a high percentage of diamond substance in it, a very rare ratio found in mines around the world.

The Commander at the base got greedy. He thought he could take most of it for himself and live the rest of his life in peace. Here the mission changed from global duty to a selfish one! He forgot they were there to stabilize the political system of the country and to ensure the writ of the government. He wanted his men to help him in fulfilling his evil wishes and they would be benefitted too. "What happens among us stays with us. Think of your loved ones. You want to hold them and never go on another mission, right men? Let's fill our pockets, and forget about the people. It's their government's mess to resolve, not ours. The riches of God's green earth have blessed us. This land belongs to God and God lead us here to reap the rewards.

My brothers, with teary eyes, my wife is dying of cancer. I have been researching a cure for years. I accepted this mission for the money. Man, it's paying off! If we are family for life, let's take what is ours." But John disagreed, he didn't want to betray his country, and his father had brought him up as a moral citizen with solid ethical values. He had a heated argument with his Commander and left the room.

Lisa was working from home those days, the world was shut down physically and operating virtually, and COVID restrictions were imposed all around. She was not in contact with John for the past week and was feeling uneasy, there was something unusual, she sensed. Within days she became so tuned in with him that she couldn't help but text him often and try to contact him every third hour. Although she was well aware of her special spiritual abilities, she wasn't sure how she could channel those and utilize them in a positive manner. She wanted to take full advantage of her strength, her superiority over others. So, she decided to contact a psychic network online for help.

Most Christians usually didn't prefer to consult psychics as it is against God's word. She knew the scripture in Leviticus 19, which said to avoid spirit mediums. But in her particular case, she thought they were the best option considering she felt more in tune with people and her surroundings. She recognized her spiritual powers but she wasn't sure how to use them effectively. She always thought God blessed her with her gifts. After all, God controls all things. Her family was never a part of any wicked doings. So, she believed her gifts were not demonic but more of a direct connection God allowed her to have – and could remove if He chose. When calling the psychic network, she wanted to ask them how legit it was to intuitively know things. The people in her social circle were not familiar with how strong her abilities were becoming. Based on any Sunday sermon, most would disagree and likely say she should leave the unknown as unknown. But that general statement was not helping Lisa.

However, one Christian friend told her to refer to herself as being called to be a prophetess – a speaker and teacher for

God. While other extended family questioned her judgment and said if she was so intuitive then why did she fail to find the right person for herself till now? Lisa didn't have answers to all those questions but thought the professional psychics might help her. However, they were not ready to tell her anything. Instead of answering her questions, they confirmed they knew she had the gift of knowing – without her saying so. Some were confused as to why she was chatting with them. Many told her to listen to her own intuition and to journal and meditate for guidance.

They did tell her John was real, but to be careful, and to trust her instinct. They further explained her greatest gift was to consciously know things without any prior information and to feel the emotions of others. She also had the gift of dreams where her dreams spoke to her. Since her intuitive gifts were strong, they thought it best for Lisa to evolve into who she would become without guidance from them. Upon ending her psychic conversations, one psychic Shaman told her, "There are many people who practice the art of divination where bad spirits use those people to give people hope in worldly things not of God. Then the world is blessed with people like you Lisa. Those who have a natural born gift that only God blesses you with. People like you serve

God and not the world. I would call you a white witch, but your Christian kind would call you a seer or better yet a prophetess because you are meant to work for God."

Somewhat clueless, she accepted what was said, and understood her gift was a blessing. Hesitant for so many years being raised not to tune in, she felt more at peace – believing her gifts were from God. The expertise she sought was not meant to help her. She was led to a path of self-discovery that was the way most of her kind learned.

Back on the base, John was stressed. He knew the combats he fought so far were against prominent enemies but now the enemy was within their own lines. He was standing shoulder to shoulder with them and knew they would stab him from the back, waiting for the correct time. So far, the mission was accomplished, the troops were able to retrieve enough diamonds and the communication system was restored. He wanted to talk to Lisa, she was his stress-relieving pill, he thought to himself. The idea of talking to her brought a smile to his face and he realized she was becoming indispensable in his life.

He called her, and she instantly picked up the phone and bombarded him with questions, "Where had you been John? I was so worried; I hope all is well?" John decided to confide in her. He briefly explained his job nature to her and told her about the cyber-attack. At that moment, the teenager inside him was aroused; he wanted to impress his girlfriend! He started bragging about how smart and skillful he was in his field. He told her his cyber security skills were unmatchable. No one could ever break his firewall. Lisa listened to him in awe as he told her it was all due to his expertise and his unbreakable firewall that the soldiers were able to reach the enemy's hideouts, counter the rebels' attack, and capture a few of them. The hackers attacked the firewall again and again but couldn't penetrate it, John made the difference otherwise they were as strong as the Agency.

"You know John you have so many personal things too, do you also have a personal firewall? I would love to learn and can you teach me how to do all this?" Lisa asked him. "It is a magical world my beautiful Lisa, it's like the data is flowing in the heavens all the time, and the key to reaching it lies in the hand of only one person who owns it," he explained to her. He told her how he was often posted from one base to another and also had to stay in weird places for days on missions, so he couldn't carry all his stuff with him everywhere. It's like an external hard drive he could access anywhere, anytime. He managed it all by himself, controlled it, settled what should stay in it and what should be removed, and he was the only one who knew the password to it.

He told her he didn't trust anyone with the server, only what he did himself. He would be ruined and finished if he ever lost it. He had stored everything in it, his weapon designs, methods of becoming an extraordinary cyber security expert, his secret files, his financials, his photos, and videos; it had all his life within it. "Whatever I make is unreachable to everyone in this world but I can reach any device all around anytime I want. This is what has made me so important for my Agency and they do not want me to leave," he added. "So, you mean NO ONE can access your data even the Pentagon! That's crazy, I always thought no one in this world could ever hide anything from them."

"No one means nooooooo … one babe except me." Lisa felt proud, her First-Class man being so extraordinary in real life, "Silently she said, this is why I named him First-Class, I knew he had the supreme talent to be the best in the world, she giggled."

They talked and talked for hours, fueling themselves with their growing love for one another. "My leave has been approved and I will be leaving soon for home. I have already told my mother and Charles about you, Lisa, I want to introduce you to them in person. They would like to learn a lot about you because they know whoever I would choose now would be someone extraordinary!" Lisa was delighted and believed in everything he said. "And then I'll fly all the way to Georgia to meet the love of my life, my Sunshine!" he added. With all those sweet future plans they hung up, promising to one another to stay in contact daily.

John goes to the lab and sees the Commander standing alongside the lab technician. "I granted your early leave, smirking he said, I'm glad to send you off!" He wanted him to leave, as he was the hindrance in achieving his evil targets. In the last meeting, they had a huge fight over the same issue. John, still upset, punched his Commander in the face and quickly grabbed a soil sample for evidence as the lab technician helped the Commander off the floor.

The Commander was worried. Having John against him met no way to help his wife. The Commander shouted as John walked away, you're going to regret this, John!" Upon leaving the altercation, John was hot like fire. Compressing his fist, he walks to his room to ease his mind. The flashbacks were starting again, and John did not want to hurt anyone. His mother calls. She wasn't well and was missing him. There were business issues too, which needed immediate attention and action. His mother was old and emotionally broken after his father's death. She couldn't take care of the business.

On his return, John had a long list of tasks to be done. He had to find an efficient attorney to assist him in selling his jewelry stores. He was anxious to sell. The sell of all three stores was worth millions. It would be more than enough to care for his mother and purchase property in America.

There he planned to build the home of his dreams and achieve whatever he wanted in his life with Lisa. As soon as his leave was granted, John was all set to leave. The Commander was happy, the hindrance in his plan was removed, and he was now free to achieve his selfish goals.

The base was located fourteen hours away from the nearest town. He left in the middle of the night with a soldier who was supposed to drive him to town. On reaching there after a continuous tiring drive he fetched his traveling documents from the embassy. The soldier accompanying him asked him to take a break during the journey but John said it was important to rush to the embassy before it closed for the day. He had a room booked for himself in a decent hotel. On reaching the embassy, he confirmed his flight and then sat in the desolate lobby pulling his laptop from his soil-filled backpack.

The jar he took from the lab cracked against his laptop during the long-rugged journey. Caring less with soil-shimmering hands he anxiously accessed his RAS. There he added the details of his recent combat and the ill wishes of his Commander. Taking a breath to put on a smile, he prepared to call Lisa.

CHAPTER SIX

Hatched

Closing his thoughts in prayer, John felt he was one of the most satisfied men on Earth at that moment. He was well in time for his flight, managed to collect all the important travel documents, and was all set to leave for his final destination. Back home, his attorney was waiting for him. He had already completed all the necessary paperwork for the sale of his business and the buyer was also in place.

John had all the plans mapped up in his mind, buying land, building a home for his family, and leading his ideal life. His mother needed him back home as soon as possible. She wasn't able to handle the stressors of everyday life. The grief forever changed her. She became more emotionally fragile and forgetful. It appeared she lived only because her body kept her alive. Her soul longed to be with her dear Ande. Now the time had come, she would pass on all the responsibilities to John and would live a relaxing life. John, on the other hand, was willingly ready for the new change, it seemed all the pieces of the puzzle were falling into the right place for him.

He was going through his travel documents to check if

anything was missing. While reading the list of the required things, he was stuck at a point; it was written the traveler must carry $950 with him. John never knew about that new rule. He was in a remote African country where the political situation recently changed. The new political government had introduced a law where travelers who wished to leave the country were supposed to carry a certain minimal amount named a traveling fund. The situation left him in a fix. He was in a foreign land where he didn't know anyone who could help him. In fact, he couldn't think of anyone in the whole world who could lend him the amount immediately to ensure he took his flight back home.

He decided to talk to Lisa about the situation. Though he hated the idea of asking the love of his life, there was no one else he could confide in except her, he thought. Ah, he sighed inwardly repeating, "trust and faith." Back at her home, Lisa was in her happiest mood, sipping wine from her favorite crystal glass and making sweet melodies about John:

"I've soared high and low

Babe, don't you know

My mind is realizing

How we were met to be

It's just you for me"

The phone rang, glancing at the number, she knew who it was. Joyfully answering, she sweetly sang on the phone, "Hello, it's just you for me?"

John was sitting at the edge of his bed, and at that moment in his life, he desperately needed her comfort. "Yes babe, all my life!" he chuckled and popped an air kiss. "Ahhh, I needed this babe." Standing to her feet, Lisa could sense there was something he wanted to talk about. Something disturbing, something worrying, she didn't want to believe her instincts at that moment. "Hmmm, what's wrong, my love?" John remained silent and did not answer her right away. He was hesitant, how would he break the news to her about his troubles. He wasn't sure how she would react.

He breathed deeply, leaning forward on the edge of the bed as he took off his hat. All his actions showed how deeply concerned he was at that time. Lisa waited patiently for him to speak; she could only hear the sound of a ticking clock in John's hotel room. Twirling her hair, she tried to figure out what was the reason that took John so long to open up to her. "Well John, I think you've been upgraded from a jungle to an old village, I've not heard of a clock like this for years. I'm here to listen to you babe when you're ready," she told him while walking to the kitchen table. She made herself comfortable by sitting in the orange oval chair, tapping her feet to the beat of the ticking clock in John's room. The night air was thick and full of frustration. Slowly John said on the phone, "Lisa, I am not what I told you I am."

Nervously clutching her hands, Lisa encourages him, "Go ahead babe, I want to hear everything from you," she told him. John started to warm her up by sharing the details of what happened to him the day before. "You remember I told you I was a weapons engineer, well I am also a part of a tactical force team," he started telling her nervously, hesitating each moment with fear Lisa wouldn't believe in him and leave him. Lisa seemed to be clueless about him and wanted him to share more details about himself. But he knew it was time to discuss the secret sides of his life to her, he had to gain her confidence.

He told her how he had a fight with the Commander and left the base in a hurry. He explained to her the grave situation at the base, how the mission went wrong, the Commander's betrayal of his job, and how difficult it had been for him to reach the town. Lisa realized he was much deeper in the agency than she thought he was. John went more into detail, sharing he had mostly been undercover, never disclosing his identity of being an agent for the United States government. He told her as part of his job, he had learned five different languages. Wherever he went on a mission, he would blend so well with the locals there that no one ever found out he wasn't a native of that place.

He told her he stayed undercover in Egypt for a mission as an Arab and once in Spain. He briefly explained to her his role as a spy in the Agency and also as a part of the tactical team. Leading up to the African mission, he tells her he loves her in all five languages, first in his most fluent tongue Dutch, then in German, and in Arabic, Spanish, and in Malay. Then he seriously said, "Babe I believe trust is earned and I am sorry I could not be upfront with you."

He paused and told her all the truth about the sirens in the background when they last hung up at the base. He explained to her how frustrated he felt when he had to kill several men for the mission and in the end realized all that went in vain because of the Commander. John asked her what were her feelings about him; she remained quiet and told him she needed time to think.

After talking to Lisa, John was frustrated as his emotions were like an entangled spool of yarn knotted up and intertwined with needles and chewing gum.

The wars he fought were less difficult than dealing with his emotional misery and having no one to depend on. He needed strong emotional support, and he was all set to start a new life, retiring from the agency and selling his business but all this drama before that was unbearable, he couldn't handle it alone. On the other hand, Lisa was concerned. She realized the man she was dealing with was far more intriguing than she thought. He was a dangerous person, not the one who would hurt her but like the ones she saw in movies, those who would retaliate in the same manner when attacked. Although John assured her, he always covered his tracks and that there was nothing to fear, she was rightfully worried. He reassured Lisa he wanted to leave that life behind and start a new, non-violent life with his family and her.

The following morning, John called her again. That was quite early; she was still in her bed. He told Lisa he desperately needed her help. To fly out of the country, the airport required each passenger to have traveling funds. On hearing that demand, Lisa couldn't help but refuse. She didn't want to trust him right away, whatever conversation they had the night before and then John immediately asking for money the next morning, all this was confusing her. She wasn't sure of her psychic ability, which was still giving her positive vibes, pushing her to believe in whatever John said but she was still unsure about John being legit. Every relationship goes through a test at some point, and Lisa hated their test was so early on.

John was hurt as Lisa was not willing to help him. But he also understood, Lisa needed time to absorb all that he disclosed to her about himself. Lisa could sense the frustration in his voice. She wasn't sure, whether what she did was right or not. She wanted to test the strength of their relationship; in fact, she didn't have words to explain why she acted in a weird manner. She was disappointed with herself too.

John's heart was heavy, he killed men for the last time and the Commander was corrupt. He was feeling lonely but he had high hopes, God would provide him help, he was sure. "Babe, God has done so much for me so far in my life. I have faith in Him; he will work it out for me this time too! I know I will soon be united with my family in the Netherlands and see you soon." Lisa told him she was also dwelling on the same. God would work it out for them. Her intuition hinted an older man would help John. They together prayed for the success of John before hanging up.

After that, John left for the airport. He was nervous, yet hopeful waiting for a miracle in his favor. He joined the queue at the checkpoint and waited for his turn. It was a small terminal and only one guard stood there to check the entering passengers. On his turn, the guard asked him for the documents. John handed over his passport and other traveling papers and told the guard he wanted to talk to him privately. The guard asked him to wait; he checked in all the other passengers and then walked to John. "Yes, young man, what do you want to talk about?" he asked. John was undercover and was dressed like a European foreigner.

John told him he was an international photographer who came to Africa to shoot wildlife. Back home his mother became seriously ill and he had to rush back. In a hurry, he forgot to carry the traveling fund and it was extremely important for him to travel at that time. The next flight would be a week later and he couldn't wait that long. The guard was a kind man, he believed in each word John said, stamped his ticket, and told him to take his boarding pass as he said, "may God be with you soldier." John glances toward the sky silently giving thanks to God saying, "come on that was you in that man. Questionably, John said, "soldier, beaming with joy, I'm a photographer." Walking up the security ramp, he takes a selfie and sees the older guard was gone from the background.

An hour later, John boarded the plane. He texted Lisa a copy of his boarding pass, assuring her he was off for the Netherlands. He had a layover in the Congo. Hovering over the North Sea, he records the magical wonder of the Netherlands. It is one of the most attractive landmasses with lush blue waves and sailboats at sea. Texting this to Lisa as he lands, both he and she are filled with excitement.

CHAPTER SEVEN

Raw

John was continuously in contact with Lisa texting her, and sending her videos, while coming out of the plane, passing through the security gate, waiting at the immigration counter, and then moving out of the terminal building. He wanted to keep her with him, wanted to feel her presence in each and every moment. Although she was hundreds of miles away, he could sense her presence at her side, he had gone deep and far in the relationship. Their energy was like a newly woven garment. Every thought and expression was tightly intertwined and hard to tear apart.

At the airport, Benjamin welcomed him. Ben was the caretaker of all his business affairs in the Netherlands. He had a special place in the family, a trusted employee of John's father who always stood by him in thick and thin. While walking out of the airport building, John's hazel eyes were dead on the target. He felt Ben was nervous about something. He was hesitant and John could sense there was something disturbing and unusual that he was not aware of. John, smiling showing all of his pearly whites, said, "Ben ole fellow, then diving in to swallow Ben with a big hug and lifting him off the ground, smiling and laughing he said, "how are you?"

As the two gripped each other tightly, John facing the street and Ben facing the Groningen airport entrance door, John still felt right about Ben's anxious feeling. Sadly, Ben chose not to be forthcoming about the store's financial status. At the time, Covid-19 hit the world hard, businesses all around were collapsing, people were losing jobs and governments were facing challenges in supporting their population. Ben felt there was no sense of urgency since John had been away from home for the last five years.

During the good years, his father had single handedly dealt with all the business affairs and successfully expanded it. After his death, Ben become the overseer and was taking care of all things. If Covid-19 did not exist, Ben would have continued doing well with the business. However, only certain jobs are for certain people. Easing out of the hugs, Ben is about to break the news – on what a terrible financial bind he allowed the stores to fall into.

All stores together had 12 employees. Two stores were closed and the third was barely operating. Few employees managed to do odd jobs for other jewelers. However, there just weren't enough funds to pay all salaries. A sizeable amount of capital was required to support the workers, it was truly a financial nightmare, a decision Ben could not make alone.

Walking toward the truck, John was still overjoyed. Ben drove Andes' favorite white pickup. With laughter, "Ah so many memories in dad's truck!" Ben tossed the keys to John. Placing his wooden cane on the side door, Ben hops into the truck. As John pulls off, he told him how excited the employees were to see him.

Everyone was together at the main operating store in the city square. They first drove past the two closed stores. John tried to remain calm by reaching out to Lisa. He texted her several photos wishing she were there with him. Communicating in any way with Lisa felt like medicine to his soul. She encouraged him to pray without ceasing. When they reached the last building, Ben gave him more news. He knew before going inside, John must know about all the drama going on there.

On listening to the details, John was shocked. The business was shut down so there was no money and they were lagging in labor expenses. For the last two years, the employees were not getting their gross salary. Each month they were being paid a portion of their total salary, with a promise next month would be better and all their dues would be cleared. But all payments seemed impossible to be fulfilled.

Without the government's hardship programs, it would have been impossible to pay any worker or debtor. John was so internally torn. No vivid emotion, just disappointment. Though he loved Ben like family, his lack of communication led John to mistrust him. Thinking back to childhood, he recalls when Ben stopped by his bedroom door to comfort John after he had gotten in a fight at school. Ben told him then, that communication is key to any problem. Now Ben was choking on his own words. Always being quick to calm down and override a situation, John snapped back to reality as he prepared to reassure the staff, he would pay them something before he left the country.

Entering the front glass doors, a young female employee greeted them with a pleasant smile, "Hello Mr. Watts," as she gestured cheerily to Ben and buzzed open the door leading to the lower level. The employees standing at full attention circled Ben as he introduced John to the staff and all eyes turned on him. They bombarded him with questions and blamed him for all the problems they were facing because of the outstanding salary dues. Few were behaving humbly but most of them were furious shouting statements,

"I have children to feed."

"Why didn't you plan for bad days?

Another, "He's rich, what does he care!"

It was difficult to handle them but, in the end, John succeeded to convince all and promised he would solve their issues as soon as possible. He asked if everyone would return the next evening. Shaking hands and confirming all will be well, a calm presence overcame John as he internally thanked God for helping him calm his irate staff. He understood their anger but also felt the honest sincerity of all his employees. In such a time of world distress, his employees remained loyal, and he wanted to financially thank them as he prepared to sell the business.

While exiting the back entrance, John had mental flashbacks of all the times when life was good. He glanced over to his dad's favorite wooden bench. Walking toward it, he recalled many past conversations where his dad supported Ben mentally and financially. As he slowly sat down, he recalled how Ben was his dad's, right-hand man. He always kept his father informed about everything from his deranged uncle to the latest jewelry trends. Ben was the most trusted person and was like family.

However, immediate financial distresses lead to negative emotions. He did not know whether to trust Ben or view him as a traitor. Internally speaking, "Why did he not tell me before now?

Was Ben trying to sabotage the sell of the business?" "No, but yes, it was of course Ben's fault. He panicked in the tense situation and did not make the right decisions. Ben is still good. Weak-minded! But, a good man." Having to face all the music alone. He looks into the clear blue sky and shouts, "You got me God! You got me."

Before coming to the Netherlands, he had perfect plans and was in a frame of mind he would easily go sell the business, buy land and a house, marry and live happily. But now all things were turned upside down. All the sugar was on the floor and money did not grow on trees.

Then, here comes Ben again with more bad news, walking behind John and placing his hand on his shoulder, "John, when did you start being a Christian? Well, whatever faith you have, you are going to need it first thing in the morning."

Rolling his eyes, "now what," John said. Well boss man,

we got court tomorrow. Maybe if you carry some of that faith, the Judge will have mercy on you." John now yelling, "What court, you must seriously stop with all of these surprises."

Ben explained in more detail how they were behind on payroll taxes and administrative fees. The court appearance in the morning was to pay the fines. That if the fines were not paid, it would prevent the immediate sell of the businesses.

Travel to the Netherlands, felt like John was walking in a field of land mines. With every step of preparedness, he was being hit with information bombs. The pressure was intense. His finances were low, and the buyer of his business was in place but he had to clear the dues before finalizing the deal. Luckily, Ben had already hired a good lawyer. In a brief zoom call, John clicked well with the lawyers. They were floating all sorts of ideas to get out of this crisis but they had no alternative choice, but to go to court and ask for leniency.

Ending the zoom call, he retreated to an old hotel in the low-income district of town. When alone, he had time to think and plan what to do next. He was very levelheaded. The military had taught him to stay undercover, both physically and mentally. Years back, when his family fled the Netherlands, he was a young teenager. When they returned years back, their lavish house was turned into an orphanage and now he had no authority to sell it.

The next morning, before going to court he drove by his old house and the painful memories of that night started pouring in. All of a sudden, he remembered his father's treasure of diamonds, which he hid in the forest. It seemed his father was helping with all this. Parking alongside the road, he entered the forest and was able to find the exact location. Kneeling beside an old tree, he saw the letters his dad carved. Letters WGWC were crookedly straight on the tree trunk, he chuckled and said, "Yessssss dad, WITH GOD WE CAN!"

Then he walked three feet to the left and dug by hand about sixteen inches deep. There he grabbed his dad's vintage green metal utility box. Inside, waiting brightly was a handful of those glittering diamonds that were just enough to pay his employees and minor expenses. John was relieved to some extent knowing he could pay his workers but he was still furious about Bens' indecisive role in the whole situation. However, he overrode Ben's weakness and promised him he would financially take care of him once the business was sold.

Just after sunset, he returned to the slum hotel took a hot shower, prepared a peg of beer, and made himself comfortable in his bedroom chair. He called Lisa to inform her about the situation, he was constantly in contact with her informing her about each and every step he was taking. Secondly, at the back of his mind, he had a feeling he needed to build a strong relationship of trust with her, which felt somewhat shaken after the travel fund incident.

While talking to him, Lisa could feel he was stressed. The recent incidents have been hard to handle, first, she refused to give him traveling funds, and then the business challenges, and he was completely shut down. John said it was like a maze in which he had lost his way. Sounding like a lazy bear, "I now have the woman I want, and life is all jumbled up." Trying to be positive while needing reassurance, Lisa said, Babe! Instead of stumbling blocks, we have a mountain to move, and I am going to plant the first mustard seed.

She needed clarity on the legitimacy of business affairs in the Netherlands. Her past experiences were forcing her to ask many questions. It was difficult for her to absorb all the new details. After all, the relationship was already stressed and they have yet to meet in person.

Though both loved one another, John's love was deeper, beyond limits as he had already accepted her as his woman. It didn't mean Lisa wasn't in love with him, she just wasn't confident about their relationship yet. Everything was money, money, and more money. It all seemed like a bona fide scam where the villain could still be John. However, Lisa's intuition outweighed her negative disposition.

John needed to return home to Georgia to clear up more financial matters and return to the Netherlands for the second court date. The lawyers were only able to get the fines postponed buying John more time. Now, he was confident all would work accordingly. Talking to Lisa, upon his future arrival in Georgia, Lisa planned to meet him at the airport. Over the next few days after arrival, he and Lisa planned to return to the Netherlands together to pay the fines early and officially sell the business. Yawning and ready to crash, he fell asleep on the phone just after singing to Lisa,

Heaven Sent

Sweet Lady

You're brighter than any Jewel

You are my Diamond

My Ruby

My Jewel of Jewels from God

Lisa joyfully said, "I am baby, I am yo girl honey! Jumping out the bed, "Ooh wee, singing like that, you forever GOT me!"

Sweetly and softly, "my man, my super, First-Class…man!" She ends the call with a kiss and John said, "Good night my Womannnnnn."

CHAPTER EIGHT

Scrambled

John struggled to sleep that night. He tossed and turned wrestling with his dreams. His subconscious mind placed him on a football field. He tackled his team and the opposing team to get to Lisa who ran circles outside the field.

Though his clothes were soaked in sweat when he woke up, he felt refreshed knowing meeting Lisa was only hours away. The first thought that came to his mind was of course what Lisa must be doing at that time. He could imagine her sleeping soundly in her bed and could even feel the softness of her black beautiful hair spread over the pillow. Smiling at his imagination, he texted her his flight schedule. The flight was good to go for the next day. He wasn't taking a direct flight but had a six-hour layover in South America, about a night stay at the hotel.

Before leaving he briefed Ben about his schedule. Ben seemed to be a little worried, he wanted John to stay over and settle things in the Netherlands before leaving. But John told him he had some other plans. Going to Georgia would help solve financial issues further.

His flight was quite early the next morning. He hurriedly

gobbled his sandwich and gulped the mug of coffee; he didn't want to be late for his flight. The cab was already waiting at the hotel gate and it took him directly to the airport. The flight was smooth and when the plane landed in South America, it was late a few hours before midnight. The airline's transport took him to the hotel where he chose to spend the night.

When he called Lisa that night, she seemed to be a bit lost and worried. John could sense that in her voice. "What happened Babe? Is everything alright?"

"Oh yes, I'm fine, can't wait to see you, come soon and right on time Mr. First-Class!" she chuckled on the phone, trying to act as unmoved as possible. The reality was, Lisa was also having dreams, but more disturbing dreams for the last two nights, and she could apprehend something bad was coming their way again. She didn't want to share her dreams with John, he already had extremely stressful days for the last week and Lisa thought she should be more optimistic and act like a sympathetic companion at that time.

The next morning, he was back at the airport to catch his flight to Georgia. Everything was well under control and John was immensely relaxed. Before checking in, he thought he must get some more cash from the crypto money machine; he may need it during travel.

Keeping his bag on the ground next to the pillar, he took the cash from the machine, turned back, and walked to the pillar. Suddenly a man with his luggage trolley coming from the other side crashed into him. All his things fell from the trolley. "I am extremely sorry, I didn't see you coming," he apologized. "No problem," John smiled back and helped him gather all his belongings. It hardly took five minutes.

Picking up his bag, John walked to the security gate, showed his traveling document, and entered the airport terminal building. The scene inside was the usual one, passengers walking for check-in, alert airport security guards scanning passengers with their probing eyes, and their spy dogs sniffing at the luggage.

John kept his bag on the luggage belt, the guard shoved the body scanner at him and he walked to the other side. There he saw two dogs sniffing at his bag, before he could get hold of it, guards approached him from both sides, and tried to take him by his arms. John was startled; he couldn't understand why they were treating him in a strange manner. Angrily shouting, "What are you people trying to do, may I know please?" "I'm afraid Sir, we need some information from you before you leave," one of the guards answered.

John ignored him and tried to grab his bag; at that moment around ten men surrounded him and tried to detain him. John was full of rage by that time; it took him hardly five minutes to smash the guards to the floor. As John stood centered, the guards look like swatted flies on the ground.

The situation seemed to be out of control and the security staff called over the military police to help them. On their arrival, the guy who was their head officer realized John was not a simple man. He had a strong muscular body and the way he punched the guard surely indicated he was no ordinary street thug. The skilled defense fighting style indicated he had military training and he should be dealt with care. As usual, John was traveling undercover and they couldn't figure out what military branch he was listed with. The officer approaching him explained the situation and told John they found cocaine hidden in his bag. That was absurd; John was clueless and shocked at how that could happen.

He convinced John to go with them for some interrogation; he couldn't leave the country before that. They took him to their interrogation room for further inquiry. Meanwhile, John's mind was continuously working, analyzing who could have planned that scam for him. He wasn't able to relate it to anyone else but his Commander at the base with whom he had fought before leaving. He must have placed that trap to get rid of him.

But in reality, things were not that simple. The setup happened because of his ex-girlfriend who was part of a Colombian criminal gang. Years ago, she stole John's money and John took custody of their son which was not acceptable to her. Like the civilized world, these gangs also have some work ethics. They consider all the members as a family and protect one another's rights. So due to that reason, some members of that gang spotted John at the airport and recognized him. That person was a local of South America, a place where everyone knows something about everyone. He prepared a plan to malign John and teach him a lesson for betraying his gang member.

The person who crashed into John with his trolley was a part of that plan. It was in those five minutes, that he skillfully placed cocaine in his bag. John was in a different mood at that time, indulged in thoughts of Lisa, and was in a hurry to board the plane so he wasn't focused to figure out something notorious was going around. Now he was paying the toll for letting his guard down.

The security personnel along with the members of the interrogation agency took him to the investigation room. He was charged with smuggling drugs, they told him. They asked him some questions and also did the lie-detecting test but he passed all tests with ease. He was a tough guy who had gone through all these tasks hundreds of times before. He viewed, the people interrogating him as kids playing for him.

At that time, they already started feeling he wasn't the real culprit but the problem was all the proof was against him being caught red-handed. They told him he would be kept under house arrest until cleared. They were not sending him to the prison but to the detention center situated in the compound next to the investigation center.

So, after an hour he was shifted to the detention center. There he started to work out how he could come out of this problem. He was still undercover and his job description wasn't allowing him to reveal his identity. For almost a week, they kept him detained in the center and kept on interrogating him every now and then. The officer in charge told him he must contact his lawyer for help in his native country. John had hoped this government had a corrupt judicial system, wanting money versus human slave labor. In preparation, he asked his lawyers in the Netherlands to borrow funds against two of his stores; he might earn his freedom by only paying a large fine.

The fine amount did not matter. It was like hell for him living there, he was confined in a small compound, completely cut off from the outside world, eating crappy food and sleeping in bunkers with some other unhealthy people. In his first hearing before the judge, he realized the lawyer provided to him by the government was not able to get him out of trouble.

He was so thankful he met the lawyers back in the Netherlands. Through their contacts, he found sufficient legal help and advice. John was good at reaching solutions to problems, he did maximum community service in detention and established good relations with fellow convicts. He knew those things would help him get out of there, community service would add positive points to his profile, and people around him would act as witnesses for his good behavior during his stay in the prison.

During his stay there, the ray of hope in the dark was the conversations he had with Lisa. They were the fuel for his attempts to get out of that painful place and Lisa supported him in his efforts and also advised him when he was stuck. John had strong willpower but sometimes those back-to-back challenges broke him. That was a real test of time for both of them. And in those gloomy days, he texted to her, "God's gonna make a way possible for us, I believe, I hope, I will hold on strong."

The good news was that John's lawyers were able to arrange funds for him. He was well prepared for the next hearing. With the sale of his stores, he had collected the required amount of $200,000, obtained character certificates from fellow witnesses, and earned enough points by doing community service. A day before his second hearing in the court Lisa told him her dream.

She said, "There will be an old man with gray and black hair who will let you go. When you meet him, convince him with all your ability that you are not guilty. Tell him how important it is for you to return back home. Your mother wasn't well and your young son is waiting for your return. She told him to a plea like a baby. To let your strong shell break so the Judge could feel your emotions.

John texted back to her, "Thank you Babe, but I'm nothing without the strongest pillar in the world (YOU). Yesssssss, you are my strongest pillar now on which I can lean in difficult times."

The next day when he reached the court, the space was

already jammed packed. There were case hearings back-to-back, the guards with him told him that was a common scene after the weekend and sometimes they had returned without meeting the Judge. That day was not good, John thought and he had to return back without meeting the Judge with an appointment after two days.

And when he went again after two days, he was surprised to see the same judge in the seat as according to Lisa's description. He showed a lot of compassion and decreased the fine to only $35,000. Another thing went in John's favor that day; a guard from the airport also came as a witness in John's favor. He explained how the camera footage of the airport showed a time when John was helping a person gather his things from the floor, someone could be seen behind the pillar, fidgeting with John's bag. That was the moment they suspected when that person put cocaine in his bag.

Then came the interrogative officer with all the test results. He told the Judge all results show John was not the kind of person who could smuggle drugs. He appeared to be a lawful foreigner that couldn't do anything illegal. They concluded John was not guilty and must be released from the detention center after paying the fine. Listening to that, John thanked God and called Lisa to give her the good news.

Lisa was so happy for him; it had been a month since he had been detained in the prison. She was having different innate feelings about him. Sometimes her sixth sense would signal her that he won't be able to get out of trouble but later she would get positive vibes in her dreams. Those things kept her faith alive in God and she became more and more spiritually strong.

She always believed everything happened for a reason and that one-month was painful but it brought both of them closer to one another, and closer to God. They had a heart-to-heart conversation with one another, Lisa would comfort him and they got to understand one another more and more. Once Lisa texted him, how do you see the role of the man and woman – do you feel a woman should be submissive and what is submissiveness to you?

Those words brought a smile to John's face, "My babe got bible questions," he murmured and texted back. "Wow. This is a whole topic on its own, lol. It is like a deep sea of discussion in itself, lol. But I'd ask first. Should submissiveness really be from the woman? Good women are naturally submissive but are men submissive? No. We are naturally egotistical. AS MEN.

And then he added, "Submissiveness to me, hmmmmmmm, is knowing your better half is way below you, probably financially or otherwise. But you decide to stoop down to the same level in order to dismiss inferiority feelings or worries. I'd sight an example. A woman makes way beyond her better half but decides to forgo expensive / better things (cars, jewelry, properties, and so on). She stoops down to using the same level of things as her husband in order not to cause inferiority worries in him. It also could not relate to material things at all. It could be a humble and unresisting obedience to one's spouse."

And then they had a lot of their time to discuss themselves and their future life. It was around midnight. Lisa could not sleep, wondering about her First-Class man. What life would feel like to have John in her arms daily, to build a future? Lisa texted him before going to bed, "Babe, have you thought about how we'd begin our life together?

And John answered just before daybreak; "I sincerely want God to be the Omega since he's been the Alpha of US. I don't think there's any sense in engaging for a very long time, however, I want us to set a beautiful future in motion for ourselves and let God's will be done. Whenever you're comfortable with the families meeting is great, but I want to meet everybody already, smile emoji, and kiss emoji. Charles and especially mom wouldn't stop talking about you whenever we talk on the phone. I remember mom telling me – she sounds like a good woman. If you lose her, well I don't know if there's any chance for you, lol. I took those words to heart. Also, I want you to be able to decide on how we're gonna kick off our family. Everything that is best for you babe."

Lisa was in awe of John. Every word he spoke was like a dream. That morning she talked with God, "It all seems too good to be true. Did you send him God? You mean - I finally fell in love with the spirit of man. Not his flesh - but with his spirit? I finally got a man that loves my spiritual being and not my fleshy body. Ooh, wee! Lord, John ain't never even been to a place of worship, but he not only read your word, but he also digested it and knows it very well. He gets me, Lord.

I feel like we have been set-aside for each other. He is no uppity self-righteous man. He is a natural born-again man who understands how you have delivered him. He is humble. Thank you; father God, for John, and thank you for my spiritual gifts and what you have allowed me to know.

Forgive us, Lord. As we humbly submit, direct our paths

father God. Ooh wee, Lord. I am gone do this right – no sex before marriage. Have mercy, now. We gone talk right and walk right. Thank you for giving me another chance to get my life right. Amen, Lord, Amen."

That afternoon, John paid the fine; he was all set to fly home. The detention center in charge informed him he would be leaving shortly, depending on flight availability. John was anxious to leave but he wasn't feeling well.

He was a healthy man and very rarely got sick. Unfortunately, he had eaten unhealthy food for days and the quality of air around was bad. All this caused him to develop serious digestive issues. He was having constant, regurgitating hiccups, and the night before his flight he had a terrible cough.

Feeling ill and restless the whole night had him worried about his health. He thought wow, now that the country is preparing to remember the faithfully departed, he didn't want to be a soul remembered on All Souls Day. Grimacing as he looked at the city preparing for the festivities, he felt like he was still stuck on the road to misfortune never wanting to be left behind in South America.

Finally, freedom was within reach. Before embarking on

the plane, he called Lisa. She was worried about his health as he was continuously coughing and hiccupping. Lisa was apprehensive; she said maybe you got a new COVID-19 virus.

John laughed aloud. He already had it twice and was among the first batch of humans to get vaccinated so he was confident he was safe. People at the airport gave him a worrying look whenever he coughed or hiccupped. John thought they must be worried he was about to spread a new virus here.

As two flat-faced guards were escorting him to the plane. John was extremely delighted; he involved them in humorous conversation and took them out of the tense situation. He was so playful like a big kid playing hopscotch, and then Lisa shouted something out of nowhere!

"John, I don't know why this is on my mind. Maybe it's another premonition; I don't know – Babe, you listening? Babe, remember my email address, if something happens to your phone and you lose my number; you can always email me. Remember! John! John."

The phone connection was breaking up. She could hear the sounds of the airport where flights were announced. John shouted at the speaker, "I love you, my Sunshine!" "I love you too, Mr. First-Class! Just before the call dropped, she shouted into the speaker, "Remember John, save my email address."

Buried on her sofa, she thought why did she ask for that at the last moment? Why was her intuition signaling John would need that information in the future?

CHAPTER NINE

Breakable

The flight was well on time. Soon John boarded the plane, kept his cabin luggage in the compartment above, and made himself comfortable in his seat with the two guards escorting him. Whatever he endured over the past several days seemed to be a nightmare for him and he didn't want to remember those haunting moments.

It was terrible, almost as bad as being captured by a deranged enemy. He never knew a gang member who knew his child's mother planned that conspiracy against him. With so much confusion on how it could have happened, he was just relieved to have his freedom.

Now after facing so much, he was finally flying home to America. During detention he told the authorities there he was a part of the American military but never disclosed he worked as a secret agent. He was a citizen of the strongest country in the world and the government made all the efforts to escort him back safely. The two-action hero looking guards traveling with him had the responsibility to protect him throughout the journey until he reached Washington, DC.

Sitting in her home, Lisa was trying to find connections between all the events that happened so far. She no longer needed confirmation of her gifts from other unknown psychics. Always caught in the dilemma of what the bible says, she thought it best to ask God for answers, as she did not want to open any unknown spiritual doors, she could not close.

Thinking back on many life events, she was led to rely more on her intuition and began intensely focusing on her relationship. They were always planning their future together. She felt the spiritual realm had bound her to this man. Clueless about the exact purpose, she felt she was there to help him evolve and experience true goodness.

To have hope that true love is possible. To understand that true love is pure love. And, that a genuine person will love the person unconditionally. That his wealth was in his heart not his bank account or his military abilities.

His personal traumas sadden her deeply whenever she thought of how much John had endured in his life. She always assured John she would stand by him so long as he stood by her. That no matter the situation, they would lift each other up when one falls down. She knew he spoke genuinely; she enjoyed being with him in conversation. His laughter, his voice, and his joy, all gave her the real taste of a happy infinite love life. Finally, they both were experiencing true love as pure love not tainted by lust.

The thought of God uniting them always calmed her spirit. She was mesmerized by how similar their painful struggles were. Instead of questioning and pulling away from God, they both grew closer to God in their adversities.

They both believed in a higher power and that the God that created this world must have had a hand in allowing them to meet. For the first time in their lives, lust did not solidify a relationship. John had a fancy for beautiful women with athletic body types.

Lisa recalls him saying how unhappy he was in many of his past relationships. At the beginning of his military career, he lusted for the appearance of a woman. Sex was fun and easy to obtain, but a strong sexship led to detachment and discontent. "Lisa – do you know why I chose your profile? I don't care if you are a size 2 or 14 or 18 or 22. I don't care about those things in life now. A Godly woman is what I need. I want to build a future on a spiritual foundation."

Her thoughts have her soul smiling over their many past conversations. Sinking into her couch, "Wow, thank you,

Lord." Indeed, they had an unbreakable spiritual bond where their spiritual love for each other wove their souls together knitting the better of two people.

Missing John dearly, Lisa prayed hard for his safety and for their future. She knew John would reach his destination by the evening of the following day and would connect to her as soon as possible but she was still dismayed.

Now, it had been a week since John reached Washington and he hadn't called her. Her younger sister Marwella called to inquire about John. At that time, Lisa was extremely worried but she always kept her cool in the presence of others.

She tried to talk normally to her but Marwella could sense the concern in her voice. She always said she knew Lisa better than herself. Marwella suggested she should meditate to calm her emotions. Lisa giggles, "yeah sometimes Marwella, you do know me better than I know myself."

It was around 7 am in the morning. Lisa pulled back the curtains in her living room, and as she learned over several weeks, light plays a special role in her spiritual power. She was always a light baby. Some children need total darkness to sleep, but not Lisa, darkness was never safe.

Even in her adult years, she still slept with a night light on. The light was and is her comfort. But now it has become her power. When she meditated in any sort of light, she would envision and tune into things better where images slowly appeared and became clearer the longer, she concentrated.

As the sun rose brightly that day, she sat on her shaggy floor rug with her back flat against her lime green couch. Her legs were loosely stretched forward, as she relaxed with her hands resting at her sides. Thinking about John she could conceive he was alive but it seemed he wasn't as well as he should be.

She couldn't exactly figure out what was wrong with him as her judgment was clouded. But she could clearly feel the truth in him. Whenever she tried to tune in, her head would tingle intensely like a rush of rippled waves. And at that moment, the tingling sensation was unbearably strong.

She saw John picking up an object and at the same time, she saw Marwella fixing herself something to eat. It was terribly confusing. When she was completely focusing on John, why did she see Marwella in her meditation? Never before had her visions been so vivid.

She called Marwella and asked her if she was really fixing herself something to eat. Marwella told her she was doing exactly the same thing Lisa saw. Finally, she thought. A good solid confirmation to believe in her spiritual gift, even more, she rushed Marwella off the phone.

She decided to pray for answers and as soon as she ended her prayer, her cell phone rang. It was John calling from Washington. "Where in the world you have been babe, can you imagine how worried I was for you?" Lisa asked him restlessly.

"I know love - you were waiting for me. In South America, there wasn't any time limit, and we talked for hours, but here in America, things have changed. I have limited time for myself. It has been one conclave after another."

Patiently listening with the cell phone buried up against her ear, it was difficult for Lisa to digest a time limit in America. She was used to having long conversations very often with him and now he didn't have time to talk. She knew he was in some kind of trouble, but overlooked the seriousness of it.

Maybe the government wasn't allowing him to connect to

anyone. With all of the background noise, it seemed he was kept under guard, probably locked in a room and cordoned from the outside world, which was the worst she could think about. Lisa could even hear a heavy metal door closing in the background during their brief conversation. It sounded like John was in a very secure and protected building.

John tried to assure her he was safe. The military had him in a safe facility on lockdown, but the virus was still spreading and more mutating strains were surfacing.

She interrupts, "Babe?" But John does not immediately acknowledge, he continues talking as if he is at a military check-in sight where the caller unloads information and then ends the call.

"Remember I had a bad cold when I left South America, so they have put me in lockdown for my safety. They want to make sure I don't catch any new variant of Covid-19." He reassured her he was healing. His cough was better and he was improving but Lisa had some uneasy feelings about him. As if he was in some kind of prison.

"John Watts, hey Mr. First-Class go to the back of the plane," she jokingly interrupts to get his attention. She feels rushed and her thoughts are unorganized. "Are they treating you well? Have you heard from your Commander? When will they release you?"

John pauses, it was hard for him to override her voice. He wanted to have a dialogue, but couldn't. Everything was rushed and watched at the base. Switching his mindset, he hides his emotions and tries to calm her down. The sort-all-talk-and-you-listen method was way off the mark of their relationship.

He didn't want her to be worried about him. He told her he would be coming home for Thanksgiving. Lisa was relieved when he authentically answered. John told her he would soon leave Washington and reach home to meet her.

Placing her on mute, John asked the female guard for a little more time. "Babe, we are going to have a great time. I am anxious to meet you and all of your family."

Lisa replied, "Do you have a large dining room table? Ahhh, everything is so rushed. I know, pacing the floor, we said we'd cook dinner at your house, but babe, Washington has thrown us off course. You should relax not entertain other guests."

John said, "Sure, sure, whatever you want. But the way I feel about you Lisa has me weak wanting my womannnnnnn.

With that magnetic smile and sensual voice, we will need a chaperone."

Lisa, feeling the intensity of his words, laughed with him, "yesssssss, so true, every day I want to be wrapped around you," the sound of many kisses flowed from her luscious lips.

John, firmly replied, hmmmmmm, then we will discuss marriage soon. Babe, what we have is so beautiful to me. I truly want God in the center of our lives. I am so thankful I got you and you got me."

In all that sensual excitement, Lisa had an uncomfortable feeling pinching her heart. In America, she felt more distant from him than from South America. There was an unknown feeling of being far away from one another, never meeting, and not talking much.

Mentally, she tried to fill that gap, tried to find that missing link in the chain, which would lead her to John. Suddenly she heard a woman's voice in the background, saying John's time was up. Lisa quickly said, "We got each other, Love you much!" John wanting to say more slowly hung up.

With a heavy heart, John handed over the phone to the

120

guard standing beside him. He had so much to share with Lisa, but so little time. Her voice gave him contentment. It assured him he wasn't alone; someone was always with him, praying for him, longing to meet him and be with him. He started recalling what happened during the whole week after he reached the base.

It was evening when the airline jet landed in Washington, DC. It didn't take much time at the immigration counter and custom clearance as he was traveling on his official passport. There were uniformed security personnel waiting for him to take him into custody.

They informed him he had to undergo some investigation before he returned home. From the airport, he went to the interrogation center at the military base where he was supposed to stay for some days as a part of the protocol. He had been in the detention center for some time and as a rule, he had to undergo a thorough medical checkup too, to ensure he was indeed healthy. Unfortunately, he still continuously coughed and couldn't breathe as well.

On reaching the base, he settled in his assigned room. After showering, he was taken to a room where three men in blue suits were waiting for him. They offered him a seat placed in front of their table, all three of them sitting on the opposite side.

"Welcome home Mr. Watts; it's been a long time. Good to see you again," one of them said. John nodded, glancing at all of them. The elder of the three men said, "The Agency keeps you busy. You Agents forgo much of your lives. The work you do is not taken lightly and we sincerely thank you and applaud your efforts." All three men then stood to salute John. John stood to attention with a humble heart and reciprocates the salute.

Upon returning to their seats, with nervous getters and clammy hands the youngest man opened John's file. As he explained the need for the last meeting, "Sir it is an honor," repositioning his glasses, "We would like to hear the details of the sequence of events from Africa to South America."

The left side door in front of John opened and entered Dr. Burke, John's psychiatrist at the Agency. Carrying a folding chair, he casually walked toward the three men and sits next to the youngest interrogator.

"Hi John, no worries, this shouldn't be long." Seeing Dr. Burke made John feel uneasy, and the entire situation became more worrisome. John knew Dr. Burke must have been called there as an onlooker, to observe his behavior during interrogation, he had to figure out if whatever John was saying was true, if he was telling each and every detail and not intentionally hiding information.

The interrogators started bombarding him with questions from all around. Familiar with his classified file; they questioned him about Asia where Phillip died, then about the rebel attack in Africa and the fight with the Commander. Dr. Burke interjects, "What led you to leave the base in Africa?"

John flashes back to his stay in South America. He ripped apart the Africa ordeal; concluding the mission was never about political peacekeeping, but more so about the diamonds. Not knowing whom to trust, he is inwardly seething, and sarcastically replied to Dr. Burke. With a piercing expression, "What? The Commander did not inform the Pentagon?"

Dr. Burke begins typing into his cell phone. Another asked him to recall what happened in South America. It was obvious; someone had laid the trap for him and placed cocaine in his bag. John simply told them he couldn't remember anyone who could have done that to him.

Dr. Burke was perplexed by how John allowed himself to get set up. "You are one of our elite Agents. You were trained to evaluate and secure any perimeter within seconds. Eyes in front and eyes back at all times. Who has your attention? What happened John?"

Then they started asking him about the days he spent in the detention center. Who were the witnesses, who helped him get out of there, how did he manage to develop such a good relationship with them that they guaranteed he was a clean man ethically and morally?

Those sequences of events were unbearable for John. Thoughts of Phillip, the corrupt Commander, enemy list, and revealing Lisa became too stressful. Suddenly, he had a nervous attack, his face became pale, he started rubbing his chest, could hardly speak, and fell short of breath.

He almost fainted in his chair, Dr. Burke rushed to him and patted his cheek, "Hey John, are you alright." John couldn't answer, his head was spinning and he was panting and sweating profusely. "Call the medical unit immediately, tell them to get a stretcher for him, he has to be taken to the hospital!" he shouted at the guards.

CHAPTER TEN

Shaken

Next was a rush. A constant rush. It was a non-stop flurry of doctors and other personnel dressed in medical garbs doing this and that. Their colleagues immediately understood whatever they shouted almost incomprehensibly. John could not make out a single face among them. His vision was blurred and his head was spinning as he got dragged along in the gurney.

His breath was an altogether different matter. They had inserted something in his mouth just before covering it with a mask to help him breathe. With every single breath he took, John could feel the pain in his body. It was almost like heaving in pain, but being unable to move. John had seen episodes on TV where doctors would try to perform CPR on patients on these stretchers where they would straddle them, but there was no need for that here. So, why, he asked himself, did he feel like the weight of the world was on his chest? It was not like he was trapped under anything, was it?

He was shifted to the hospital situated inside the military base. John had been covered in blankets, sweating profusely, and he tried to constantly call a nurse to help him rid himself of the blankets, but that only made him ache more and feel cold again.

Half the time John could not make himself lift his eyelids. They felt too heavy. Every time he closed his eyes it felt as if a weight had been lifted off him. John could feel something thumping, but it wasn't his heart. It was the pain.

It was like an emergency light, John thought—it was the first thing that came to his mind as he focused on the pain. Those things that light up, flaring for just a second, before dimming down and starting the whole process again. That was how his pain felt, like a constant wavelength of ups and downs.

Time felt almost floaty, with the days coming and passing with John never really realizing *when* he was there. Sometimes he dozed off, and it was dark outside as he woke up. Other times a nurse would wake him because it was time for him to eat again. A doctor would come by on occasion, talking to the nurse, but John could never remember what he said. The doctor would not talk to him much except for a few encouraging words. John could not even remember what those words were most of the time.

Several weeks passed before John's condition had

become stable enough that he would regain his senses and his complete consciousness—enough for him to be able to talk with the staff stationed at the base.

The doctors stabilized him and performed many tests searching for a diagnosis. They told the officers it could be an attack of asthma but they needed to rule out any serious issues.

In South America, the air was much worse, hanging over the throat. It felt like an itch that no amount of coughing could scratch out. So, the doctors thought he must have developed allergic asthma due to pollution. But the test results they received after an hour signaled a grave situation. Due to intense pollution and unhealthy living conditions, John's heart did not receive enough oxygen to work efficiently and he was suffering from cardiovascular disease. As a result, one of his arteries was completely blocked and another was about to be the same.

The doctors advised immediate open-heart surgery to prevent further damage as it could be a threat to his life if not treated immediately. The decision was left to John; they also asked him if he wanted to call anyone in the family, any immediate relative in case the surgery did not go well. John thought of Lisa but he didn't want to burden her more. She had already suffered a lot of emotional stress because of him.

In a short span of time, since the start of their relationship, Lisa was mentally supporting him continuously during all his testing times. This time it would be very difficult for her, it was a matter of life and death for John and he felt they meant the world to each other. Deciding not to inform even his mother, he gave the doctors his consent for the surgery.

On the day of the surgery, he called Lisa from the patient's room. Lisa was so happy to hear from him. He wanted to talk his heart out to her; he wanted to share with her what he was going through. She was his pillar to lean on.

He wanted to tell her, "I've been very sick babe, the pain is very bad, and I'm in the worst state. It seems all this was waiting for me to reach the USA, I found out after reaching here that I had developed a cardiovascular disease due to a polluted environment and unhealthy diet. I am scared to death; I don't know if I will survive or not. I desperately need you by my side, holding my hand, walking while walking beside me when I would be going to the operating room. I need you, to comfort me, to assure me that everything would be fine and we would be together soon.

But this was all he could say to her in his imagination and

never say it aloud to her. Instead, he told her, "I won't be able to make it home for Thanksgiving Babe, I have to undergo some additional medical treatment and as soon as I become better, I will get back to you."

He couldn't speak much; he had uncontrollable emotions and he could feel a lump in his throat. Previously he thought he would feel better after talking to her, but now he felt even worse extreme loneliness. He regretted each and every moment of being away from her, how much he wanted to be there for her for the holidays.

He didn't want to lie. But this lie was good for their relationship otherwise Lisa would get worried for him. Lisa wasn't aware of his surgery, and till then the situation was out of sight out of mind for her. John ended the call after five minutes. Before hanging up he said, "I'll love you forever, you are my strength!"

Lisa felt his passionate remarks throughout her body. John shed a tear as he thanked God for what he had and then thanked Lisa for having faith in him.

CHAPTER ELEVEN

The Dinner

It was late November and Thanksgiving preparations were in full bloom. The radiant sky, crisp weather, and the lure of foliage colors of fall, all added to the beauty and joy of family gatherings. The cold was welcoming, too, though some days got *too* cold to be appreciated.

The Christmas decorations were already up, as Lisa noticed quite often. The year had passed almost as if January was last week, but for Lisa, the days were passing by slowly. After talking to John, she should have felt better but that was not the case. Her psychic ability was stronger and she was now signaling something unusual, something she felt uneasy about.

Unable to rest, Lisa sauntered each room through her home distracting herself from reality. She washed and folded every piece of fabric from clothing to dishcloths. Her home was so clean it smelt like a clorox factory. Her pantry was now arranged in alphabetical order, something she wanted to do months ago.

By noontime, she started repairing the chain on her mountain bike when Rachel called. "Lady, what are you doing? Ann needs your help in the kitchen. Dinner is at 4 pm! We needed you five hours ago."

Lisa replied I'm, huh, getting ready now. Hearing her distress, Rachel switches to her big sister-mom voice, "Don't make me come drag you over here. You ain't even met John face-to-face. Keep it moving sister girl, keep it moving. You got two hours to get here. Ann is about to drive me crazy – thinking she remembers how to make your famous mac-n-cheese and cornbread dressing. Lisa, are you listening lady?" Feeling annoyed, Lisa rolls her eyes before saying, "Yes ma'am." Rachel replied, "You got two hours, now, love you Buttercup."

Poor Rachel is in the kitchen with Ann and Marwella. They'd been cooking since early morning. Even now being a grown adult, Ann still can't handle cooking Thanksgiving dinner alone.

The first year their families united, Ann was surprised at how well their late mother and Madear trained the girls to cook and bake at such a young age. During their first Thanksgiving as a blended family, the girls cooked everything, except the Turkey.

They left that for Ann and she of course served up a dry

bird that crumbled like sand. Over the years Ann always tried her best to perfect meals to their taste, but holiday dinners were still a fun challenge.

Lisa was imagining the worse on her drive over. While reminiscing the good ole days and feeling upbeat, she jammed to her music, electric sliding in her seat as she wrapped her car around the front entrance. Though she wanted plans to include John, those thoughts took a backseat when several nieces and nephews ran out to greet her. The entire neighborhood heard the kid's auntie Lisa chant, "Buttercup. Fluff it up."

Preacher-Man was at the door with arms wide open to welcome her in, "My Buttercup is home!" Ann, shouted out from the kitchen, "Lisa baby, you just in time." Her brothers Si and Lee simultaneously look and jokingly say, "You already know."

Lisa, wraps her hair in a bun, stomps her right on the wooden floor, and rolls her neck as she asks, "Huh, where are my hugs?" The twins jump up from the recliners, each lifting her up with a bear hug.

Pulling away to look up at the twins Lisa said, "Now that is what I'm talking about. So, how is business? Si reports,

"All is golden." Not able to sit and chat, Ann and Rachel come to drag Lisa to the kitchen.

Rachel is stirring the collard greens. Marwella is preparing fried corn. A few nieces are making aunt Wonda's famous potato rolls. Madear is too old to stand and sits at the breakfast table near the sunroom.

Madear had already made the cornbread for the dressing. Lisa greats her with a gentle hug and kiss then picks up the cornbread. Madear placed her hand on top of Lisa's hand. Her blue eyes aligned with Lisa's brown eyes.

Lisa knew she intuitively knew something, but avoided a conversation with Madear by commenting on how good the cocoa cream moisturizer worked, "Madear, ooh wee, your hands feel so silky, ain't nothing better than a woman with silky skin at age ninety-five. You gone have all the single men lined up outside." Madear smirked and said, "Later child, later."

Hours later, the entire house smelled like a southern gourmet kitchen. The young children set the table with white plates trimmed in gold and matching gold silverware.

Each sister brought out her dish to the table and placed them in the center of the table. Keeping heritage and tradition alive, the food was displayed using elaborate antique serving dishes made by their enslaved ancestors.

The men poured homemade grape juice into each crystal glass. As each person stood behind his or her chair; all nineteen of them, joined hands. Madear sang a short old hymn and Preacher-Man prayed.

Lisa was relieved no one drilled her about John. When Madear had another chance, Lisa was getting ready to leave when she motioned for her to sit next to her on the porch swing. She said, "Be careful Buttercup. I feel something is wrong.

Sometimes things have different meanings. I raised you well. Remember what I taught you and never not follow your first thought. God is good to us all the time. When confused and powerless, let God direct your path in all things. Yes, child, LET GO and LET GOD.

I dreamt of you just yesterday. You were in a cave surrounded by rising water. I now see your emotions are scattered in many directions. John appears to be good, but a wolf lurks among the sheep." Interrupting, Lisa replies, "Madear – what you say now, I's gone be alright." Madear rolling her eyes, "there you go, brushing off what I say."

CHAPTER TWELVE

Yoked

A men! Amen! Praise the Lord, Brother Barnes glorying God just before shouting, "be the light! Hold the light!" It was the first Sunday after Thanksgiving and Lisa was absorbing every sermon on TV that morning. The whole week she missed John immensely, but life was going on. She so much wanted to connect to him but couldn't find a way.

At her kitchen table, with her bibles spread across the table, she was watching the Sunday service online flipping the channel between two favorite Ministers, one being her dad, Preacher-Man. The notification icon on the corner of the TV screen blinked. "A new email, I'll look into it later," she told herself. It blinked for the second time; Lisa glanced at it and sprang into her chair with excitement.

It showed the sender was John Watts! Looking toward her vaulted ceiling, she raised her hands in prayer. "Shouting, thank you, God, for answering me." She eagerly switched the screen to her email inbox window. As she read the e-mail word by word over and over again, she sat there in disbelief. Life has once again bluffed her! John wrote,

"Good morning to you. I sincerely can tell you I don't

remember who you are. But, please listen. I go by the name of John Watts and reside in Georgia. I am currently at a military base in Texas. The staff informed me I am a high-ranking soldier. I, unfortunately, developed a cardiovascular disease that plunged me into surgery in November. The surgery went well and my heart is in great condition. However, the surgery led to an increased risk of having blood vessel problems in my brain.

As a result, I was in intensive care unconscious for over 6 weeks and developed amnesia. Physically, I'm in the process of recovery now and a team of specialist work with me daily. But in spite of having a great medical team, my life remains a mystery. Right now, I am like a newborn baby with zero memory, one whose brain is blank like a white slate longing to absorb information.

When I sleep, I am watched. They hope my subconscious would recall something. Apparently, they know I have an external drive. They claim I used the drive to retain everything about my life and life's work but I don't remember my passcode.

I was only able to find this email as an emergency contact from my iPhone. I know you must be someone important and dear to my heart. My iPhone screen is broken, so I have no facial recognition to access my contacts. Please, please help me. I guess you are the only one who can tell me who I am. Without the passcode and without your help, I may never know who I am. Whoever you are, please reply."

All the joy turned to sadness for Lisa. John cannot recall even the faintest memory of their affectionate and amazing relationship. "So, this was the reason why my brain was signaling me something worrisome was coming my way," she told herself with a cold sigh. "I managed to get in contact with you through the email in my emergency contacts list the day I came here. I have an external drive, which contains all my life memories, and my work details, and it's the key to helping me return to my real self. The problem is I couldn't remember its passcode. Without entering that code, it's impossible to recall who I am," John wrote.

Hours later, she is mentally stuck chopping through the email over and over as she recalls certain past conversations with John. So that was the end of the talent he used to flaunt, Lisa thought. The secure drive of which he always bragged about no one would ever be able to hack was now like a treasure chest of a lost kingdom with a secret coded lock and with all the wealth locked into it! His entire life achievements, all his special memories related to him, his family, and his dear friend Philip, and most importantly all the unforgettable moments captured in pictures of Lisa were all gone. Lisa knew he was reluctant to open up to her.

In the beginning, for him then, she was a stranger. He wasn't disclosing everything, hiding information, like he had a double life. Aside from nicknaming him Mr. First-Class, she jokingly called him Agent 009. Not knowing the intricate web of all John's stories, she was definitely a part of the silky web he spun. Every signaling vibration met something. She was so unsure if he kept her email address. To know it was vital like this was emotionally overwhelming. "Huh! Amnesia! Really!"

"I am contacting you because I could only find this email in my emergency recovery contact. This guided me to ask for help from you because I know you must be someone very important to me and dear to my heart. Now I do not have access to my old email address, messages, or text. Please, please, please I guess you are the only one who can help me find my identity, take me to my destination of self-awareness." Lisa kept on reading and digesting every word over and over, tears rolling down her cheek. And then he wrote, "I go by the name of John Watts, if you know me, please respond to my email, I would be waiting anxiously for your reply, probably this is my only hope to return to my world. Thank you as I await your response." Lisa was distraught. She still believed in John and needed answers.

She already went through the phase of wondering if he was a scam artist, and now it seems like he could be. But the details of his life and what they shared over the past months were more real than what someone could cruelly fabricate. Is this for real? Is He telling the truth? She sent him an email, "Dear John, I am speechless. This is Lisa. We met a while ago on ZoZo Match. We started talking by phone in January. We talked constantly. Our conversations were magical in supporting each other mentally, especially when you were in South America. Though we never met in person, we spiritually fell in love and started planning a future together. It's been many weeks since we last spoke in November. Where in Texas are you? So many questions, please call me!"

Within seconds of her sending the email, her cell phone rang. On the third ring, she answers, "hello." John nervously replied with a meek tone, "Lisa?" There is dead silence. He said again, "Lisa?" "Can you hear me, it's John. John Watts. Lisa, please say something."

His voice is still sexy and masculine. His accent still captivates her. Pulsating sensations run through her spine. The reality has finally come; she thought about what to make of the moment. Her mind is like a billboard, advertising John's last words before her. She does not want to lose contact with him ever again but is afraid that their life experience has expired.

Hoping to connect and meet him in person, her voice cracks as she replied, "Yes John I'm here." Teary-eyed, "I missed you so very much. I prayed for this moment. It's still hard to believe, we are finally speaking."

John loves the sound of her voice. He is faintly smiling, as her voice is still very soothing to him. He interrupts her, "Lisa, you sound so good, so sweet. I feel something just listening to you. I don't know how to explain it, but it is something. Awe Lisa, I can honestly say, I want to remember all of you." By her tears, John felt she was honestly someone special in his life, but who was she exactly? He asked her to tell her about their relationship. Lisa wipes the tears from her face and takes a deep breath.

The importance of the call was the one chance she had to possibly meet John in person. She explains about his son Charles who was in boarding school. Knowing the government would have a record of that, stating such was her hope that John would believe the words she spoke.

She rattled off, his actual home address, which is something he would have never divulged to anyone. She felt like she was on a witness stand where knowledge of John would set her free to be with him. Leading up to the external drive, she mentioned the Commander incident in Africa.

Undisclosed in the beginning, Dr. Burke is in John's room listening to the call. Mentioning West Africa prompted John to interrupt, "Lisa, I see you definitely know who I am. Your connection to me is highly important. In the following protocol, our conversation is being recorded. I apologize. The sincere sweetness of your voice gripped my emotions. Again, I apologize for not stating this in the beginning."

In recovery, the Agency informed John about the indecent in West Africa, but he could not make sense of the report. Agents are sworn to secrecy, but his love for Lisa had John breaking every code. Lisa was his love and is now a liability. The sudden acknowledgment of being recorded did not faze Lisa as she anticipated their distrust.

Free to speak, John informed her about the entire situation and what he was going through. The external drive was his life force. Controlling the situation, Lisa lied to him. She told him she had the password and would only tell him in person.

Silently becoming impatient, Dr. Burke interrupted. Grasping John's shoulder to politely quiet him, he took over the conversation. He informed Lisa that John was a genuine and very trustworthy person.

He confirmed the legitimacy of the surgery and reassured her John was now safe. He asked Lisa to assist and welcomed her to the base. With her plan in motion to see John, she accepts the invitation. Dr. Burke didn't waste time; he informed her a chopper would arrive at her home within hours.

Lisa sat unmoved for a long time after the phone hung up. The situation became intense. She never knew his password. Now obtaining her wish to see him was more important. She began meditating trying to make connections, but all visions were blocked.

She tried to clear her mind, to think of other things, but to no avail. She could not figure out if her mind's eye was closed or if it refused to open.

The disassociation of John's reality left her clueless and helpless. Knowing John's past and having insight about the Agency meant full control. That no matter her decision, knowing too much was never good. Once again, she stood with her man. But she stood blindly.

Rushing to pack a few things, she called Marwella and briefed her about the situation. Marwella was worried, she wanted to come to her immediately but the chopper was landing in her backyard. Lisa reminded her of the Apple Air Tag they used when traveling. Marwella could sync and track her whereabouts this way. By doing that, at least someone would not be kept in the dark like she was right now.

So much has happened and so much was said, and it had Lisa bravely curious. The only way to close this chapter was to open a new one in Texas. Marwella was apprehensive; it could be a trap for her. She told her she had no fear.

Waves rippled in her pond as the chopper landed. Lisa hung up the phone sending a kiss and I love you to Marwella. There was no time for her to answer.

CHAPTER THIRTEEN

Hawk

A young handsome man dressed in military attire approached her at the back door, his frame towering over her much shorter one.

"Are your Lisa McDaniel?" he asked. She showed him her license. He then took her overnight bag and led the way. Walking down her backyard steps she almost tripped on the broken stone step. Hearing every movement, Lisa could feel his shadow as the soldier turned around to catch her from failing.

Things just got real. The chopper was so loud. In shock he even heard her trip, she thought this man must have eyes in the back of his head to hear me stumble in my comfortable shoes. Looking into his luring green eyes, she nodded to herself, knowing that she would be fine with him. He sensed her fear and told her she was in good hands. She tried to study his face as she walked next to him, trying to memorize it.

Helping her into the chopper, he secures her seatbelt and placed a headset on her head for hearing. The chopper smoothly lifts off. She looks back toward her beautiful home like it was the first day she moved in having to restore its natural beauty. "Ma'am are you ok?" the pilot asked. She said nothing. Glancing at her from the rear-view mirror, he broke his silence. "It's a short flight. John will be happy to see you."

Her beauty captivated the pilot. He could not stop looking at her. Her soul was an open book. Confidence, beauty, and success radiated a sweet spirit. The pilot makes eye contact with the mirror again, "John is a lucky man."

Upon landing, the area was extremely remote. Not a town in sight for miles. The base was in the middle of nowhere, just mountains, and water. Buildings were scarcely visible. Lisa prays for insight. Her emotions were a mixed cocktail. She was happy John is legit but fears the secret Agency.

The pilot she recognized as green eyes formerly introduces himself, "They call me Hawk." He lifted her off the chopper by her waist. "It was a pleasure being your pilot. Perhaps we'll meet again. Now the entrance is straight ahead. Follow the road to your left."

A very flustered Lisa listened to his instructions, stealing a few glances back as the pilot turned back around to enter the chopper.

CHAPTER FOURTEEN

Delicate

S eemed like her carry-on was rolling faster than she walked. The distance from the chopper to the entrance was short but felt like miles away. Every step seemed heavier than the last, and she felt her knees weaken. Was she having a panic attack, or did the road suddenly seem all too heavy?

Screaming inside, she must have fixed her blue coat a thousand times. A few more steps beyond the bridge, she looks back taking mental note of how steep the drop is from the bridge to the river canal below.

Facing the entrance stood two uniformed soldiers and outcomes, Dr. Burke. Cameras that circled the complex already took photos from every angle. She cleared facial recognition with ease. However, his greeting her was more business than welcoming. Even he was overly curious as to whom the woman was that emotionally connected with John.

No form of technology was good enough for Dr. Burke, not when it came to observing and quickly analyzing Lisa's body language. "Welcome, Lisa. I see you are just as anxious to meet John as he is to meet you."

Grabbing her carry-on, he hands it to the receptionist and reaches to cup her hands between his hands. Looking down at her he said, "John has made significant progress. His memory loss could be short-term. I will take you to him shortly. In the meantime, Rebecca will escort you to your room. I'm sure you want to freshen up first."

The building is extremely secure. Rebecca is in the center of the circular entrance area. Security cameras are strategically placed. Rebecca is an older woman with an athletic build. She is short like Lisa, but her presence is mighty. Lisa feels she can trust her more than Dr. Burke.

A doorway opens behind Rebecca's desk. She escorts Lisa to a small quaint room with, a typical military-style bed and a basic bathroom with a shower. She sets her carry-on on the table and then attempts to text Marwella, but there is no signal. "Duh, I should have seen this coming. Why would there be a signal? This place is like an elaborate high-tech prison compound with modern décor."

Worrying less about the loss of cell signal, she gets ready. Dr. Burke soon knocks on the door. Lisa slowly opens the door. Dr. Burke politely compliments her. She smells of fresh roses and is refreshingly beautiful. As they walk toward John's room, she realizes she was only a few feet away.

This confuses her greatly. Their connection was so strong when he was thousands of miles away. Now within a few feet of his presence, she senses nothing. As she thinks, Dr. Burke is steadily talking. He reminds her to let John lead the conversation. "Though John has made progress, different triggers could set him back." Standing in the hall outside John's room, Dr. Burke backs up and allows Lisa to enter.

Opening the door gently and upon entering the room, "John," she called his name in the sweetest tone. Standing near the bay window around the right corner from the door, John is eagerly waiting.

The smell of her rose perfume had his heart pounding with excitement. As she graced the corner, he stood there still in welcoming attention. Their eyes locked, he is everything and then some. Lisa is living in the moment. The photos he shared did not compare to his physical presence. He is so much more handsome in person and gently strong towering over her curvy frame.

She equally fascinates John. Lisa is so beautiful to John. He is naturally attracted to her and swiftly approaches her to swoop her into his arms. It's as if a spiritual force was pushing them together.

They tightly embrace. The connection is a natural urge of togetherness where their souls are communicating with each other beyond their flesh. The message of never letting go settles deeply in them both. Lisa feels all his energy. Her mind and body are overwhelmed with emotions. She left herself weak in his arms as if they have known each other for a lifetime.

There are no words said, only warm embraces and gentle magnetic kisses. Tears of joy streamed down Lisa's face; she couldn't believe the moment arrived.

John's spirit knows he knows her. He is sparkling with joy, but his mind is not catching up fast enough with the sequence of happenings.

His brain was buzzing. Fragments of past conversations appeared in bits and pieces. He was behaving like a kid guessing his Christmas gift, "You are my babe, yes babe, church girl, wife to be," he muffled in her ear. Standing firm, she held him tightly as if saying she didn't want to lose him now.

After passionately swallowing his mouth with a kiss, she whispered in his ear, "Remember you are my First-Class man!" John got overwhelmed with emotions; he is shedding tears of joy because vague memories are resurfacing. She licked a teardrop from his face kissing each cheek and wrapped herself deeply into his arms as they passionately smothered each other pressing against the wall with each tongue thrusting kiss. Her energy is medicine to his soul. She wants all of him in her.

Clothing and cameras hinder physical ecstasy. John lifts her up into his arms, but suddenly stops knowing all eyes were on them, he gently places her down. As her feet touch the floor, his hands trace over her curvy backside, with joy, he says, "My Sunshine! Yes, my love! My wife to be. I remember this spiritual connection, wanting only you."

Their steamy union was so intense, it became difficult for Dr. Burke to watch from a distance. He too was not alone. His was accompanied by a retired Commander, his father, Mark. As Dr. Burke began to leave the video surveillance room, Mark said, "Well done son. John loves quick like Ande. My brother was always a wuss for pretty women. We will use her as bait." Dr. Burke uncomfortably nodded and says, "like father like son." He then proceeded to John's room. Before entering, he briefly stood outside the door. With his ears alert, he jiggled the doorknob to signal he was entering.

Lisa and John were so intertwined they did not feel his on-looking presence. Dr. Burke announced himself by clearing his throat. Lisa looked up at John submissively and whispered in his ear, "I do not trust him." She then moved to the left side of John, straightening her coat over her dress, fluffing her hair, then holding John's arm tightly.

"Well Dr. Burke if it's ok with you, I would like to extend my stay." John nodded in agreement. Dr. Burke, "Yes, of course Lisa. Your connection to John is most beneficial. Astonishing! We will discuss the arrangement in the morning. John, how do you feel?"

Feeling a little drained, John replied, turning toward Lisa, "She is my missing link." Walking toward the door to exist, "Very well. We must let you rest now," said Dr. Burke. Before leaving the room with Dr. Burke, Lisa leaped up to hug John and held him tightly while softly whispering in his ear, "the impossible is possible - pure love is our true love! John gently touched her face with both hands and kissed her forehead. Lisa then whispered, "Babe, a challenge is coming. We will pass it together."

"He who finds a wife, finds a good thing and obtains favor from the Lord."
Proverbs 18:22

———————   ———————   ———————

"Love never gives up, never loses faith, is always hopeful, and endures through every circumstance."
1 Corinthians 13:7

ABOUT THE AUTHOR

Georgia is my home state. I believe every moment in life is precious. Laughter and making memories are good for the soul.

For many years I dreamed of writing and sharing stories. My fictional work fuses life experiences, dreams and imagination where nothing is met to be perfect. Everyone digests elements of a story according to their liking. Some get it and some don't. Some critique and some praise. Whichever you are, thank you for reading this book.

In the meantime, I'll be reminiscing on shared experiences as I work on my next great book. Thank you for buying Woven! You can find me online at: www.SeFeSel.com